Praise for Sven

T0247117

"Like all great writers, Sven Popovic is not only a master storyteller but also a conjurer of atmospheres. Reading this book is like hanging out with friends during one of those long and dreamy European summer days, where night and day eventually merge into each other and you are taken in by the subtle surrealism of youth. A book, yes, but more importantly a powerful experience."
— Carlos Fonesca, author of *Natural History* and *Austral*

"Sven's stories are not burdened by reality, as much as reality isn't burdened with our generation. It's hard to talk about generations, but if there is a cohesive thread that binds these forever-post-forever-inbetween people (who, instead of Proust's Madelaines have toilet seats of rundown bars), Popović found it. These stories are permeated with melancholy and irony, they wear a tired sneer that never goes into cynicism, and they ask the following question: who is that 'we' that we talk about? This is literature that dares to do what a lot of contemporary fiction shrinks away from—dream."
— Lana Bastašić, author of *Catch the Rabbit*

Other Work by Sven Popović

Loser by a Landslide
Mali i Levijatan

Sven Popović

LAST NIGHT

Translated from the Croatian by Vinko Zgaga

DALKEY ARCHIVE PRESS

Dallas, TX / Rochester, NY

Deep Vellum | Dalkey Archive Press
3000 Commerce Street
Dallas, Texas 75226
www.dalkeyarchive.com

Support for this publication has been provided in part by grants from the National Endowment for the Arts, the Texas Commission on the Arts, the City of Dallas Office of Arts and Culture, the Communities Foundation of Texas, and the Addy Foundation.

THE ADDY
FOUNDATION

Paperback ISBN: 9781628975000
Ebook ISBN: 9781628975260

Library of Congress Cataloging-in-Publication Data

Names: Popović, Sven, 1989- author. | Zgaga, Vinko, translator.
Title: Last night / Sven Popović ; translated from the Croatian by Vinko Zgaga
Other titles: Nebo u kaljuži. English

Description: Dallas, TX : Dalkey Archive Press, 2024. | Series: Croatian literature
Identifiers: LCCN 2024012069 (print) | LCCN 2024012070 (ebook) | ISBN 9781628975000 (trade paperback ; acid-free paper) | ISBN 9781628975260 (ebook)
Subjects: LCGFT: Short stories.
Classification: LCC PG1620.26.O68 N4313 2024 (print) |
LCC PG1620.26.O68 (ebook) | DDC 891.8/336--dc23/eng/20240506
LC record available at https://lccn.loc.gov/2024012069
LC ebook record available at https://lccn.loc.gov/2024012070

Cover design by Daniel Benneworth-Gray
Interior design by Anuj Mathur
Printed in the United States of America

Contents

"*We'll never get a book published.*
We're not nearly serious and frustrated enough."
—Zvonko Karanović

"*To be serious is to be impotent in the face of the world . . .*"
—Antun Šoljan

ROOTS AND BONES

You've been chosen as an extra in the movie adaptation of the sequel to your life.
—Pavement

I realized early on that I stood on the wrong side. Those on the other side would look at me, point fingers and whisper. At first it was unpleasant, but in time, like an animal in a zoo, you get used to being observed. Sooner or later you stop reading their lips, realizing that they never say anything smart anyway.

There is more space on the wrong side. I can spin and flail my arms unafraid that I will bump into someone. I can sing my heart out and whistle and nobody will care. Living on the wrong side gives me the right to say that everyone else is wrong. And so, I regularly do.

I think I'm happier than the othersiders. I think that, despite being misunderstood, I get by better than they do. People on the other side don't talk to shadows or trees. Shadows and trees have a lot to say; they've been here for a while. Our shadows know us better than anyone, and the shadows of other people are full of whispers and secrets we promised not to tell.

So, what now? Is this a story about magic and the time when the sky was still young? Every day, thousands of people burn down their childhoods. But for me, I'm born again with every blink.

I'll go back to where this story started. As kids, we gave names to trees. In our eyes they were alive, they were our link to the sky. Through the treetops we watched the pieces of the big blue streaked with clouds and planes, and every one of us had their own corner of the sky. In the meantime we grew up, we forgot the names of the trees, the trees died and the sky was no longer ours.

A DREAM OF FIVE CITIES

Everything seemed so close
As if the angels' wings of Berlin and Zagreb
Were touching
                        —B. Čegec

THE CELESTIAL TWO

Viktor is gone, reads a note written on a yellow Post-it someone left on my door. *Viktor is gone, find him any way you can.* My eyes slide across the office. The office I share with Francis. We never clean it. Two tables, one across from the other, covered in heaps of paper, mugs, empty boxes of takeaway food, two computers, and two lamps. Around the tables, cabinets brimming with files. We're drowning in paperwork. Next to the door, a coat rack with nothing on it—it is summer, after all. Francis is late; I guess he'll bring some breakfast. Through the cheap plastic blinds, the first waves of light start to creep in.

Viktor is gone. The guardian angel of bums and prostitutes. I think about where to start. In my mind, I sift through a list of names of all the people Viktor worked with, was close with, or had a beef with. All of them angels, second-rate prophets, lesser deities, and similar entities for whom people have long stopped caring.

Isaiah. Also known as Rale. Once, long ago, a big-shot

3

among the prophets. Nowadays he sometimes dreams about the result of this or that game and wins some petty cash off a bookie, just like all failed prophets do. That's a start, at least. I might find him somewhere around the outskirts of Novi Zagreb, in Utrine or Zaprude. I hear steps on the staircase. That'll be my breakfast, coming with Francis.

HE REMEMBERS

I remember the day I came into this world screaming, like the asteroid that wiped the big reptiles from the face of the Earth. I remember trembling when the first breath of air coursed through my body. I remember the warmth of my mother's skin. I remember the low buzz of the hospital machines. I remember the atonal melodies of the lullabies playing from the speakers in my crib. I even remember things from before my screaming arrival.

I remember all the shades of the sky. I remember the rhythm of the pulsing stars. I remember the scent of the ocean foam. I read somewhere that the trauma of birth is so intense that our first scream erases all memories of the world where we were before. With me, something went wrong. I remember everything.

I also remember the dream I had last night. I was swimming in a cold river, against the current. Pretty soon I lost my strength and started sinking, deeper and deeper, dimmer and dimmer. I was surrounded by darkness, freezing and breathless, until a light reached me from somewhere. I saw jellyfish, grand jellyfish glowing in every color. They engulfed me in their tendrils and carried me to the surface. I woke in a cold sweat. I washed my face and lit a cigarette, leaning on the windowsill. The sun was in the east, red like a newborn. Just like me when I took my first breath, just like the asteroid that killed all the big reptiles. The stars twinkled on, and the sky remained unchanged, just a day older.

I make coffee and record my dream into a large black notebook. All my dreams are in it. Francis calls me around nine. He asks me if I'd like to have coffee. I tell him that I'm having coffee right now. He asks if he can come over, he wants to talk. Even though I know that he needs something, I tell him to come. I know that he'll bring along his partner, whatshisname, Bob.

I warm my hands on the cup of coffee. Morning is in full swing. Somewhere outside in the distance, a dog is barking.

THE OTHER CELESTIAL

The coffee's good, I say, and I sit at the desk. Bob looks around the apartment, and Danijel taps his fingers on the desk.

What do you need, he asks me.

Right down to business?

He shrugs. No point in wasting time, you're here for a reason, you wouldn't have called me so early otherwise. What's the problem?

Viktor is gone, Bob chimes in as he rummages through his bookshelves.

That's none of my business, and go easy on those books.

We thought you knew . . . I begin.

I don't know where he is.

What about Rale, I ask.

Isaiah? He arches an eyebrow and sips his coffee.

I nod.

What do you want him for?

Well, he *is* a prophet, isn't he, Bob interjects again, leafing through the *Tibetan Book of the Dead*.

A second-rate prophet. Danijel emphasizes the *second-rate* bit. And a bum at that. He hovers around a bar and keeps tabs on the odds that the bookmakers are offering.

Which bar?

The Lemon café bar, near the Utrine market. Across the street from the bookmakers.

Ah well, shall we? I ask Bob. He returns the book to its place on the shelf and nods. If you see him before we do, tell him to get in touch, we might have something for him.

And what have you got for me?

The rest of the morning will be quiet, I say, and I close the door.

THEY PLAY HOPSCOTCH

I watch the fish in the tank. They change colors constantly. I blink, and they leap out of their fish-tank, fly, turn into butterflies. The butterflies flutter around the room, turning into a whirlwind. They turn into a thin girl with long black hair, wearing a pale green dress.

I love that trick, I tell Hana.

We're running late, she replies. We're late, where's the chalk?

I take a piece of chalk out of my pocket. White. Catch, I say, and toss it to her.

She catches it. I don't want the white one. She reaches for her purse on the table in front of me and rummages through it. She takes out a piece of blue chalk.

Voila, she exclaims, spins on her heel and starts drawing

on the hardwood floor. She is drawing hopscotch courts, simple, childlike. At the end, she draws a half-circle, and writes HEAVEN in it, in big letters. Let's go, she says, and starts jumping. She reaches HEAVEN and disappears, leaving behind the scent of a spring breeze and asphalt after rain. I sigh, get up and follow her. I jump, and leaping into HEAVEN, I picture myself on a school playground. I close my eyes. I open them again. Above me, blue skies, streaked with white. Beside me, tall grass streaked with blue and purple flowers. Skyscrapers and buildings pierce the sky, and we stand on hot asphalt.

You're late, Pavel says. He's leaning against a tree, looking away from us. A tall, dark-haired boy who rarely (or never, as he would have it) combs his hair. Pavel has sideburns because he thinks they make him look like Corto Maltese.

Hana becomes playful.

Oh, Sis, Sis, Pavel mocks her.

It's all Yeshu's fault. He likes to watch me transform from fish into butterflies.

I shrug. What are we going to do?

Lie down in the grass and look at the skies, Pavel says and heads toward the meadow. We follow him. He stamps down on the tall grass, smoothing it against the ground. He says it will tickle us less that way. We lie down and look at the skies.

So, what now? I ask him.

We'll try to figure out if the sky is the same color as it was when we were little.

We watch in silence. Pavel starts to hiccup. Hana and I look at him.

Someone is talking about you, Hana says.

This hasn't happened in a long while.

We turn into crows and fly to the nearest tree, to conduct our meeting in the shade. We're less conspicuous that way.

Except to this one guy who always asks us where Corto is. We stay silent, we don't caw.

THE PROPHET'S DREAM

Sometimes I dream of train tracks. In my dreams they are empty, with no beginning and no end. I never have deciphered the meaning of that dream; it just pops in from the outskirts of my conscience, caves my skull in, and leaves me to amble around like a ghost for the rest of the day.

There you go, I heard you only dreamt of match results.

I sniffed. If that were the case, Francis, I wouldn't be here, next to the market, in this bar. If I scored a ton of cash at the bookie's, I wouldn't still be stuck in this city.

What's wrong with this city?

The guardian angel of the bums is gone.

I thought you knew where he was.

I asked him for a cigarette. Camel Lights. Francis always did have style, unlike his partner Bob. Bob would smoke anything. Bob had food stains on his shirt. Bob had just gone to get a kebab.

How would I know where he is?

You're a prophet.

A second-rate prophet. I emphasize the second-rate bit. Francis is settling in, placing both hands on the table. He expects an answer.

Ask the crows, I tell him.

Why the crows?

If they know where Corto Maltese is, they'll know where Viktor is.

The crows, then. You mean . . .

Pavel and his gang. Yes.

Francis unloads some change on the table, to pay for my coffee. He thanks me and promises to find Viktor. I don't care. I'm a bum—with or without a guardian angel, I still don't have electricity in my flat. Francis heads towards the door.

You know, I speak out, twenty years ago I had this dream. Francis stops at the door. I saw old merry-go-rounds and swings, their paint long since peeled off. I saw skinny young guys debating about concepts that weren't quite clear to them. Tossing around, so casually, words like *death, beginning,* and *universe.* I saw girls high on bad weed giggling in school yards. I saw concert halls, half-empty. I saw young guys again, but these ones weren't so frail, they were aggressive, half-drunk young men, hanging out with half-drunk girls wearing too much makeup. And the Earth was rotating faster than usual. An eerie vision.

So what are you trying to say?

I feel as if I fell asleep and woke up twenty years later. It doesn't feel like anything has changed.

It hasn't. See you, Rale.

Francis leaves. I drink my coffee. I go out and watch the clouds. They're in no rush.

HE WRITES DOWN HIS DREAMS

Writing down dreams is tricky business. When I wake up, half of the sounds and colors from my dream fade. So I write them down while I'm still half-asleep, stumbling to my notebook and writing down impressions, random images, and thoughts; I let my hand glide in unison with my mind. Only later do I read what was written, and collate it, like a pastiche. Now I'm leafing through my encyclopedia of dreams, looking for the entry I made when I last saw Viktor.

It was foggy, and the streetlights looked like distant stars. I was standing all alone in the middle of a footpath on the school playground. It was cold; I jammed my hands into my pockets and started walking. I could make out a silhouette in front of me. It soon assumed color and shape: it was Viktor.

What is this?

A dream.

I can tell that much.

Why do you ask, then?

I'm asking you why you are here?

You want to know why you're dreaming about me?

Will you take a walk with me?

He nodded. Soon we were in a park. It was spring. The dream soon bled into reality. I still didn't get the symbolism.

Of course, the encyclopedia describes it somewhat differently. Something like: FOG—LIGHTS LIKE DISTANT PLANETS—SOLO—WALKING—SILHOUETTE—VIKTOR—STUMBLED INTO EACH OTHER'S DREAM—ENCOUNTERING SPRING

Old man, where have you wandered off to now?

SHADOWS AND WHISPERS

We were too careless. Careless, whereas Francis and Bob are pros, detectives extraordinaire in the service of the Celestial Bureaucracy. And here we were, in my apartment, on the fourteenth floor, between piles of books and old records. It's not that they're unpleasant or that they're going to push us around, it's just that us shadows don't like to be questioned. We know many secrets and tricks. It's no fun when others know them as well.

Where's Megi? Bob asks.

She decided yesterday that she's bored with this town, she's gone away for a couple of days. Or a couple of weeks, perhaps.

Megi is my sister. She's the youngest in the gang. She's prone to wandering. She wanders around town, through her thoughts and hypothetical situations. She has a theory that every hypothetical situation creates a new world. I told her that it's nothing new, that every possibility creates several new worlds.

Where has she gone to?

I don't know. She got on the first train out.

We knew that you'd come looking for us, Yeshu says.

And find us, Hana continues.

It's hard to miss three crows cawing in a circle, as if they're talking.

It actually is, I say as I join the conversation. Only this guy from our neighborhood noticed us up until now. Anyway, what do you need? I thought that the Bureaucracy wouldn't interfere in Shadow matters. That was the deal.

We're looking for Viktor, Bob says, staring out the window, the city spreading out in front of us, underneath us.

He's one of yours, what do we have to do with him?

We've asked Danijel. Danijel directed us to Rale. Rale told us to ask the crows.

If you can't find him in the city, find him in a dream. I'm sure that's where Danijel and Rale run into him sometimes. In dreams.

We do not dream of him. In any case, we need permission to enter someone's dream. And it's terribly impolite to go around poking into other people's dreams.

The city dreams of him. Several cities do. He has been

a guardian angel in Berlin, Münster, London, Madrid, and Zagreb.

We will need a skilled dreamwalker, Francis thinks out loud.

I think it's time for Danijel to get the hiccups. Yeshu giggles.

But he won't do it for free, Hana says.

We will, of course, need a favor in return, I add.

You guys don't mess around, do you, Bob says, still staring out the window.

We just enjoy the rare moments when the Bureaucracy needs help from the shadows and whispers.

The shadows have been here longer than us. Bob steps away from the window, shakes our hands. We're in your debt. We'll contact you as soon as we find the old man.

In Münster—Kuhviertel. Brelin—Kreuzberg. London— Soho. And Madrid—Lavapies. Those are the spots where he used to hang out, I add.

Frank nods, Bob winks at me, and they slowly disappear in the darkness of the hallway.

I actually feel bad about it, I tell Hana and Yeshu.

Why?

I would have loved to go along on that walk, five cities in one dream.

CITIES IN SHORT CUTS

Five cities in one dream? Danijel lifts his gaze from his book.

It's not impossible, I tell him, Francis has consulted the manuals.

It's not, but it depends greatly on whether you've been to those cities.

We fall silent, look at each other at the same instant.

Because, if you haven't, it all depends on how you see those cities, and that is hard to put together. Of course, we all dream of cities, we let ourselves be guided by the sound of their names. With London, it's a thick fog, pierced by yellow lights, wet pavement, and endless streets. With Madrid, it's winding, narrow streets, summer nights, and song.

What do we need to do, then?

Can you set up the dream? Francis interjects.

Sure, Danijel mumbles. He looks out the window. The sun was in the west, red like a newborn. Like the asteroid that killed all the big reptiles. The stars twinkled on, and the sky was the same, just a day older. He sets down his book and gets up, walks to his study. We can hear him shout.

Here's how it goes: you'll take a piece of paper and write down whatever comes into your head when you think of a city. Try to keep it as concise as possible. Short and sweet, got it? And give me fifty kuna each.

What do you need the money for? I shout.

I'm going out to get whiskey, he says, coming back and handing us paper and pencils.

What do we need whiskey for?

To help our thoughts flow, to help you sleep. *Post vinum verba.*

After the wine come the words?

That's right. It'll work better if you're stone cold out.

No narcotics?

Christ, why would you need those? You've got your brains. I'll be back soon; you guys start writing.

I grab a pencil and start thinking. I start with Münster, the yellow lights of storefront windows, the smell of cinnamon and the headlights.

HE BUILDS CITIES

I take a sip and watch the two of them. I close my eyes and I can hear them scribbling. They write and then cross out, correcting as they go.

Don't cross out so much, I warn them, we need whatever pops into your minds first, no matter how abstract it may sound. I can hear Bob refilling his glass. We've drunk more than half a bottle, my thoughts now flowing more freely, ideas flickering, appearing and sliding away like raindrops on a windshield. I decide against a refill; I'm okay right now, but if I have any more, my thoughts will go numb. They'll be done soon.

Okay, give me the papers. They hand me the papers, I fold them and head for the study.

What now? Francis asks.

I take a stone bowl and several bottles. Now we craft the dream, I say.

Bob studies the bottles in my hands. Arcadian dreams, he mumbles, I haven't seen those in a while.

There's less and less of it, I reply, placing the bowl, the bottles, and the papers on the table.

It looks like polar light, Francis comments. Bottled polar light.

How long will this ritual take, Bob asks.

This is not a ritual. A dream is easy to create, even in artificial ways. The key is to carry that dream over into the waking world, or carry yourself into the dream.

I pick up the papers and look around for a lighter. Bob gives me his. I light up the papers, their thoughts and images slowly burning, the ashes falling into the bowl. I open up a bottle and pour out its contents, the polar light drips over the ashes, bringing them to life; inside the dish, tiny towns, towers and cathedrals, streets and rivers sprout.

What now? Francis asks.

Now sleep, I say as I raise the bowl and blow the ash cities into their faces.

MADRID OR ANY OTHER CITY

The night was descending on the city like a spider, a hungry spider. Lights slowly came on and the buildings came alive with a yellow glow in their guts. I looked around, trying to make out what city we were in. Across the street was a run-down hostel, with a neon sign, its working letters flashing H-O-T-E-L. I noticed graffiti on the wall, two silhouettes with top-hats, bowing to us.

So, Francis starts, where are we?

I took a few steps to a streetlamp with lots of stickers on it. One of them was a picture of a bull captioned *Welcome to Spain, the only country that enjoys torturing animals.*

Based on the language, I chuckled, we must be in London.

Very funny. Where did they say we could find him?

In Lavapies, follow me.

We wound our way through streets smelling of urine and alcohol. Spaniards hung out in the streets, not in clubs like people in other cities. A song drifted in from somewhere. Sad. It must be about a woman, and unrequited love.

We kept walking, and, from the left and right of us, we could smell the scents coming from restaurants and taverns, Thai, Indian, Lebanese. People talked loudly, drank their cervezas and talked about whatever it is that people talk about. Madrid was always much louder at night. We soon reached the square, where a throng of people were sitting on the ground, drinking; we saw kids playing in the park while their parents were having yet another beer across the road from them. Some of them were rolling joints. I heard the song more clearly. A tipsy old drunk was singing about a woman he didn't love. I felt goosebumps. It wasn't the most beautiful song I'd ever heard, but it was the most honest. Painfully honest: the drunk was disarmed in front of the world.

Where to now, Bob?

We look for a café worthy of such a gentleman.

Wandering around, we found the Café Barbieri. It looked elegant, as if it used to be a regular haunt of writers, poets, and jazzmen. They still come over, but their hair has gone gray in the meantime. We opened the old wooden door and went in. The walls of the café are oxidized mirrors, to the left of the door is a cigarette machine, the bar is long, and pillars of cast iron support the roof. Jazz was coming out of the speakers. All the guests smoked, talking loudly. No sign of Viktor, however. Suddenly another melody started intertwining with the jazz, something electric and defiant. I could soon make Rotten's voice out, fighting its way through the murmur of the jazz drum brushes. Reality was cracking, melting away, and soon there was no trace of the Café Barbieri, the jazz replaced by the Sex Pistols.

I looked around; we were in a small joint with several older punks at the bar. A young couple was making out in a booth. In the corner, a vintage jukebox played only punk singles. This could only have been London. Bradley's Spanish Bar, Soho. I looked out into the street and saw a graffiti of Sid Vicious.

Toto, I've a feeling we're not in Madrid anymore.

Hell, we're certainly not in Kansas, either.

Well, let's go, the night is young.

We got out and went in a random direction, wandering around Soho, passing by dealers and night clubs. There were a lot of young people around us, straight, fags, dykes, trannies, skins, mods, punks, hipsters . . . Francis suddenly stopped in front of a night club. Dark basses throbbed from within.

What is it? I ask him.

I have a feeling he's in there.

Oh come on, can you hear that music? They're playing trip-hop or dubstep or something like that in there.

Francis pulls me in by my sleeve. Pale green lights lit up the space, no one is at the bar, and the people in the booths nod their heads to the rhythm of some Massive Attack song, sipping their drinks. It all looked like one of their music videos.

Come on, he's not here.

Francis raised his index finger.

What?

And then I heard it. The basses became even more fierce, the dark sensuality of Massive Attack became lost in the frenetic beat, the green lights started shifting colors, and the walls started to melt. Soon we were in a much messier night club, red lights dancing over our bodies, and the down-tempo trip-hop metamorphosed into drum and bass. We were surrounded.

Do you recognize this place? Francis shouts. I can barely hear him.

I nod. Club Zapata, I yell, Berlin, Tacheles. We push through the crowd to get out. I feel the sand beneath my feet; the bars outside are decorated like something out of *Mad Max*, with ironing boards used as tables.

Interesting place, my partner mumbles.

A former department store. The Allies fucked it up during World War II, and it has since served as a meeting point for artists, free spirits and other malnourished creatures. There's also a museum of metal sculptures here, it looks like Tim Burton's mind. Tacheles means *dull truth* in Yiddish.

How do we find Viktor here?

He's not in this neighborhood, they told us Kreuzberg was his haunt.

Follow me. We got out of the complex and headed for the U-Bahn stop. The characters in the graffiti came to life, Super Mario jumping alongside us, trying to grab that mushroom, get that extra life. The streetlights went wild, going on and off, painting the floor with shadows. We descend onto the U-Bahn stop, and there's no one there. The train soon pulls in.

A train? In inter-city traffic? Francis raises an eyebrow.

This is a dream, operating under completely different logic. I open the door and board. All the compartments are empty. We pick one. The train engine starts with a creaking sound. It heads off into the darkness. We can't see a thing. We ride around, unaware of the passage of time. We're silent. We patiently wait for the train engine to pull in somewhere. I can slowly make out shapes in the darkness. Soon we emerge, and I squint at the sudden burst of light. We stop. Francis and I get up and go outside. We step out onto the train station. A gust of early autumn air washes over us. It was early morning, blue and quiet.

This doesn't look like a U-Bahn stop to me.

Yeah, me neither.

Münster? I ask Francis.

It sure as hell isn't Zagreb.

We halted a cab, telling the driver to take us to Kuhviertel. We glide silently down the streets. On the horizon, the spires of churches and cathedrals. We moved through streets and seasons. It's snowing on one street, but we make a turn and run into springtime green on the next. He stopped near Pinkus' brewery, a brick house with a blue neon sign. I told Francis to pay and got out of the cab.

Do you know this town?

Barely, I spent a couple of days here before I slipped into the Netherlands. Francis slams the door shut.

A nice town, a lot of students, I'd say.

Yeah, there's a nice café nearby, they make great coffee. Brazilian, I think.

What's it called?

The Café Malik.

Well, let's go, then.

We headed down the street and soon saw the café. We walk in. A young, dark-skinned waiter is smoking a cigarette. As soon as he sees us, he puts out the cigarette. He says he can't smoke here, it's against the law. We tell him we don't mind, sit at a table, order coffee.

What now? I ask.

I don't know, we wait for a sign, we look for a crack in the dream.

The waiter serves us. Francis pays him no mind, doesn't notice that it is a different waiter than the one who was smoking. Although I merely blinked, it seemed as if I'd been sleeping for days; suddenly, we were no longer in that café, or in Münster, it would seem. We were in a much smaller establishment, the walls yellow, plastered with newspaper cut-outs, ancient articles, pictures of dead writers.

Hello, guys, I hear a voice, pleasant, mild. I turn around and meet equally pleasant, kind, blue eyes. We get up and sit with him.

Well, hello, old man, where have you gone to? Francis asks him.

I've been wandering, he answers.

More like, you got lost, I jibe.

He blinks. How can I get lost if there's no rest waiting for me at the end?

COLORED CHALK

We walked around the school playground, Yeshu, Pavel, and I. Through the treetops we saw parts of the great blue, streaked with clouds and planes, and each of us had their own corner of the sky. The two of them were stuck in a discussion about the new album by the National. I found it too soppy, thus had nothing to add. Pavel was just commenting that one of the songs sounded like it was copied off a cheap postcard from London. Yeshu accused him of being a cynic.

I listened to the kids playing and came to the conclusion that the sound of play is the same in all corners of the world. I closed my eyes.

When I opened them, I saw a bunch of kids drawing on the asphalt with chalk. Among them, I saw an older girl whose figure I recognized instantly. It was Megi.

The kids were drawing on the asphalt, and their drawings came to life. Colorful balloons and dragons flew into the sky, and flowers sprouted from the asphalt.

Pavel, your sis is making a mess again, I commented.

Yeah, I can see, but let her be; the sound of children's laughter warms the whole world.

That night was especially warm.

THE LIGHTHOUSES
ARE BLINKING

I've learned all the days of the week, the first boy says.
  We learned that ages ago. According to the other boy.
  Yeah, but Megi told me that they taught us wrong.
  So what's the right way?
  Monday, Tuesday, Cloudday, Thursday, Friday.
  Cloudday? Clouds are in the sky.
  What about days?
  Well, days are down here, on the ground.
  So the sky doesn't know what days are?
  Exactly.
  How come?
  I don't know.
  Megi, too, told me that the sky doesn't know what days are,
but that Cloudday sounds nicer than Wednesday.

HOMEWORK

I like math even though doing math has nothing at all to do
with ~~the real world~~ reality. Take my mom and dad, for example.
Two numbers, with me on the other side of ~~equality~~ the equa-
tion. And what happens when one of the numbers goes away?
Maybe later they'll teach us about numbers that don't exist.

*

Who's that Megi anyway? asks the boy we introduced as the other boy.

An older girl.

How much older?

She told me she was old enough.

You've been talking to strangers.

No I haven't. She's not a stranger. Her name is Megi.

*

HOMEWORK
THE LIGHTHOUSE

Lighthouses sleep during the day and blink at night. They tell the ships where the coast is. That way the ships know when to turn.

*

What else did she say?

That some dreams don't go away when you open your eyes.

What do you mean?

They stay on this side of the looking glass.

The looking glass?

Yes. Dreams are on the other side of the looking glass, where you recall everything. You know every language and floating comes naturally. Over there, snow doesn't have to be cold and can even be black or something. Sometimes clouds can fall to the ground, too.

And how does Megi know that?

She's a dream as well. It's just that she has decided to stay here.

You're making this up.

Am not.

Prove it, introduce me to her.

I've only met her twice. Both times she came to me while I was waiting for you on the big branch of the Little Monkey. No! On the Tree of Life. I've forgotten how the Vikings used to call it again.

Yeah, me too. Well, she might come again.

But she told me that she sometimes goes out and can't stop walking.

She'll come back, I guess.

She told me that as well. If you go straight long enough, you end up where you were. She gets bored of always being in the same place.

You've made her up. She doesn't exist.

Does too.

We'll see.

Yeah, we will.

Did you know that the Vikings never really wore those horned helmets?

I didn't.

*

HOMEWORK
MY FRIENDS

I've got ~~lots of~~ many friends. Every day when school is ~~done~~ over we have secret meetings in a secret base which is a secret, otherwise they wouldn't be secret meetings or a secret base.

We like to climb trees and everyone has their own branch and their own piece of the sky. And I also have a girl friend. Megi is on the other side of the mirror, where you remember all the things you don't recall when you wake up.

*

It's been three days and she still hasn't visited us, says the boy we introduced as the other boy.

Maybe she's wandering. She often wanders.

They sit at the same desk in school. They're in daycare. They were the first to finish their homework, and so now the teacher has to warn them every now and again not to distract the other children. The teacher warns the first boy not to flail around in his chair or he'll fall off. So what, he thinks, there are worse things than falling. The nun from his Sunday School, for example. That old cow always yelled at him. For their first class she told them to write their names on the first page of their notebooks and decorate their signatures. He drew the sword of Gandalf the Wizard, writing his name on the blade as if it were etched into it. When the nun saw it, she went berserk and started yelling—why on earth would you draw a wizard, that's pagan nonsense, throw it away and start over! The boy liked the idea of the sword, so he erased the wizard (luckily, he hadn't started coloring him in with his crayons). He considered his options. He remembered the angel with the flaming wings. She would probably like that. He drew an angel as best he could. No halo. The wings were a bit lame. But the nun liked the drawing. Old cow.

You're a liar, said the other boy to the first during recess, as they were trading football cards. Soon their parents would come to pick them up from daycare.

Am not.

Are too.

They got into a fight that day. The teacher called their parents in. Once again, Megi didn't show up.

*

HOMEWORK

Our homework is to make up a rhyme
  The moon is as shiny as a dime
  The sky is a canvass of cloud
  There's no one up there so it doesn't get loud

*

The next day the boys didn't speak to each other and wouldn't sit together. In fact, they had to be forced to sit next to each other when they came to have lunch after class. Each of them stared into his plate, gazed unflinching, refusing to glace even a millimeter to the right, or left, respectively. They didn't trade football cards. The other boy played football, and the first drew hopscotch lines on the asphalt, using a piece of white chalk that he had nicked from the nun in Sunday School.

Don't you have nicer chalks in your school? It was Megi. Her hair was still tousled. She wore jeans and a sleeveless black shirt with the picture of some four guys with long hair and leather jackets. She wore scruffy sneakers. She was nothing like the girls from his school. He liked that.

Megi! Yelled the boy. The first one.

Megi? The other boy paused, mid-dribble. They stole the ball from him and went on playing. He ran up to Megi and the first boy.

Hello, kid, Megi said to the first boy.

Where have you been?

I've been wandering.

See, I told you she was wandering, gloated the first boy.

I've brought some chalk for you and your friend. Colored chalk.

He's not my friend anymore.

How come?

He said I was a liar and that you weren't real.

Well, you said she was a dream, the other boy said. Dreams aren't real.

And yet here I am.

Yes but I can see that you're not a dream.

Tell me then, could a real person do this? And she took some chalks from her pocket: a red one, a blue one, a green one; and so on, and so on; and started drawing dragons, balloons, and flowers. The dragons and the balloons flew up into the sky, and the flowers started sprouting from the cracks in the asphalt.

And so the drawings, freed from the asphalt, became a part of the sky.

FIRST STEPS

You told me that, when everything is possible
Nothing is real anymore.
                                        —Simo Mraović

In the snow, she took her first steps. Steps that disappeared along with the snow. As if she never left a trace on this earth. She's twenty-one now, and she's not really here. I don't mean to say that she's distant, just that she's haunted by a feeling that nothing that happens to her is real. As if it's happening to someone else, and she's merely an observer. Since she felt nothing was real, she sometimes had to touch certain objects and people to make sure they were actually there, that they wouldn't melt away like dreams when she opened her eyes.

It's been twenty years since those first steps in the snow. Sometimes she feels like the days have melted away like dreams. They weren't even sequences, or logical wholes. Just Technicolor fragments. It even seemed to her that it was all a dream. During the summer she would lie on her bed and smoke. Smoked so much that the whole room was in a fog. A novel on her side at all times. Sometimes Dostoyevsky, sometimes Kafka, sometimes Murakami, sometimes Kamov. She never bothered with poetry. Sometimes she would simply lie awake, her brown hair spilling around and underneath her. She would shut her eyes and think about oceans and words that remind her of eternity.

She wouldn't go out until the sun went down. During the winter she hung around cafés. She sat alone. She often smoked an entire pack. That covered about a hundred and fifty pages and two or three cups of coffee.

She met him in college, in the middle of fall term. He was tall, slightly hunched, too smug. Loud. Always in the center of attention. But he still didn't get along with most people, his charm unhelpful in helping him fit in. In his own way, he also wasn't there all the time. He claimed that he was always surrounded with wonders, but it nonetheless sometimes seemed that he harbored romantic notions about the past. She would see him out with his friends. Always laughing. Charming punks. Rumor had it that they got together and listened exclusively to vinyl records and went only to old movie theatres. A terrible cliché, can't be true. Constantly in their own little movie, with witty dialogues and a perfect soundtrack. He wanted to be an outlaw. He seemed absolutely insufferable. They hooked up at a mutual friend's party. He caught her off guard, with the dumbest pick-up line she had ever heard.

Have you ever been kissed to a Smiths song?

She was, that night. "Bigmouth Strikes Again" was playing. He later told her that he couldn't stand them anymore. He wanted to douse Morrissey with gasoline and set him on fire.

I think you're exaggerating, she told him.

Oh come on, the guy walked off the stage at a festival because he saw a barbecue somewhere in the distance. A sworn vegetarian and all that, *Meat Is Murder*.

You're still exaggerating.

Alright, so maybe I wouldn't set him on fire, but I'd hurl meatballs at him.

How old are you?

Twenty. I think. Why?

Sometimes you sound as if you were six.

What does that make you? Dating a six-year-old.

We're not dating.

Oh really?

Yes.

We kissed to a Smiths song.

What does that have to do with anything?

It's got everything to do with it. It's, whaddyacallit . . . romantic.

What do you do?

Don't change the subject.

What do you do, Elias?

I write.

What do you write?

Stories.

What kind?

Love stories.

She frowned. Romance novels?

No. Short stories about love.

Oh.

Do you fall in love often?

I don't think I've ever met a woman I didn't fall in love with.

Ugh, what a disgusting cliché.

Okay, a beautiful woman. Who listens to good music. And watches good movies. And she has to read.

What do you read?

Cortázar.

And what else?

Poetry.

What kind?

About love. He laughed. He had a loud laugh.

How about you, what do you read, Andrea?

Don't call me by my name.

What should I call you, then?

I don't know. I don't like my name.

Why?

It's plain.

What do you mean, it's plain?

She shrugged.

All right, what do you read?

Big books.

What about right now?

2666.

Bolaño?

Sí.

He nodded. I'll just go and skip this song. The Velvet Underground. "Venus in Furs."

What's wrong with the Velvet Underground? She asked.

Nothing, it's just not exactly party music.

A friend of hers had put on that song. She wasn't too happy when he replaced it with the Strokes. He replaced the old New Yorkers with some younger New Yorkers.

Besides, why not? He said. The Strokes are just as artsy as the Underground, but they work better at parties. You designers and architects think more about posturing than about the music itself.

What a horrible stereotype, she told him.

Sometimes they're useful.

But you told me you couldn't stand stereotypes.

Stereotypes are fun as long as they're not about me.

That's somewhat hypocritical.

It's exceptionally hypocritical.

You're an unusual fellow, a walking contradiction.

It's a Zen thing.

This has nothing to do with Zen.

I like to think it does.

You lie to yourself?

I'm still wide-eyed enough to believe in things that are patently untrue.

I'm not sure if that's good or bad.

Me neither.

I think the world might be a better place if everybody was just a bit silly. But I'm not sure I could pull it off.

Me neither.

You know what?

I don't.

Baby, you were born to run.

He laughs.

Let's get out of here, she said.

Where to?

My place. I have a bottle of wine at home. I'll let you play the Strokes.

Deal.

*

They stepped outside. The moon was a tiny notch in the night sky. He told her that.

How do people forget about the moon? About all of its shapes.

I don't know, she answered. I love it when you can see its face. Like, as if it's howling, or, at the least, shocked by everything it's seeing. Like it's telling me, "Why the hell did you make everything so complicated?"

It seems like it's disinterested to me.

Oh. So you think it wouldn't mind if I kissed you right here?

It wouldn't.

You know, I'm like the moon sometimes. I watch and I'm disinterested.

I know that feeling. I know it must sound funny, but I sometimes try to make my life more like a novel or a movie.

Oh well, it's best to discuss these things over wine and music.

Where do you live?

Not far. Let's walk.

Deal.

*

The first time they made love, they were testing each other's mettle. It wasn't sex as much as it was a process of proving virtuosity. When he woke up, it was still dark. The streetlights smashed against the window and dispersed across her little room. Above her bed was a poster of Modesty Blaise. On her nightstand he could see Murakami's *Norwegian Wood* and Bolaño's *2666*.

He gets up and puts on his pants and shirt. Ties his shoes. Takes his coat and gets ready to leave. Standard practice. He stops. She is still sleeping, her arm around the empty space where his body lay just a few moments ago. He takes her cellphone and types in his number. He leaves the room silently, sending her an SMS.

Oh . . . sweetness, sweetness I was only joking
When I said by rights you should be
Bludgeoned in your bed

*

So, you guys made love? He lit a cigarette with a match. They stood outside a diner as the rain poured.

Made Love? My friend, I'm a romantic, but I don't think I've ever made love. He borrowed the other man's cigarette to light his own.

Okay, so you penetrated her?

Elias blew out smoke.

So, did you?

A gentleman never tells.

We're not gentlemen. You're an idiot, and I'm a bum. But I'm also your best friend.

Best friend? He raises an eyebrow.

Yes.

That sounds like something out of kindergarten.

Fine, you don't have to tell me, I don't give a fuck. But I won't invite you to my birthday.

He laughs. Okay, yes, we did.

Cool.

Cool.

Let's go inside, he says, tossing away his cigarette.

Let's.

They sat back down at the table. The coffee had gone cold. Elias took a sip.

Yuck.

Yeah, it's not anything to write home about even when it's hot.

They sat in silence. Elias tapped the table restlessly with his fingers. First the pinky, then the ring finger, then the middle finger, and the finally the index finger. It sounded like a horse galloping.

I'll be off. I haven't slept all that well lately, and your midnight phone call didn't help.

Sorry.

It's fine. I'll see you.

See you, Maroje.

Don't call me by my name. That's what she said to him. He remembered the poster in her little room. Modesty Blaise. Yes, he could call her that. Modesty.

The two of them will be two lines that had waited infinitely to touch, for a moment to live through an eternity together, and a moment to disappear, uncertain whether they would ever be allowed to intersect again. Two accidents waiting to happen.

And so he sits in the diner while the neon lights twitch off-rhythm, and the drizzle of the rain against the window is the only thing connecting him and her at that moment. He pats his fingers nervously against the table edge. First the pinky, then the ring finger, then the middle finger, and finally the index finger. It sounds like a horse galloping. And she sleeps. She dreams of walking barefoot in the snow. Across a snowy field when the sky is as white and frozen as the ground. The sun is faint and distant. Almost as if . . .

WE'LL NEVER MAKE A GUNSLINGER OUT OF YOU

The cracks are growing, I grow into them.

—Repetitor

I was born at the best possible time, and I've lost my shadow. It's not a thing that's easy to lose. I've been known to misplace my keys, my lighter, my notes, and my book, and I sometimes forget someone's name or a date, but nothing like this has ever happened to me. I stepped into the light and realized that the laws of physics weren't working that morning. I looked, astonished, at the place where my shadow was supposed to fall, moving my arms and legs and jumping like a monkey, trying to make nature work again.

Hey there neighbor, is everything all right? an old man asks, sweeping away leaves.

It seems I've lost my shadow.

He shrugged. It happens to every boy who doesn't want to grow up.

No, really, I've lost my shadow.

He leaned against his broom. If you want to find something, you best start looking for it, instead of flailing your arms around.

It was early fall, the leaves had just begun covering the streets and rustling under my feet. There were no clouds in the sky and the birds were singing and doing whatever it is that birds usually do. I decided not to go to class that day. I headed to the nearby bar, ordered coffee and read the sports pages.

Dinamo will lose the next game, says Rale, sat at a nearby table. They say that Rale is insane. I think he just has a different way of looking at things. He once stopped me in the street and told me I would never die, that nothing ever really dies and that I shouldn't worry. Another time, he didn't really tell me anything, he just pinched my cheek and pointed his finger at the sky.

Really? They'll lose to Rijeka?

I dreamed the results of this leg.

Doesn't matter, I don't bet on games.

That's smart—money is, after all, just paper with pictures of national heroes on them.

Why is everyone so crazy about it, then?

That I don't know. I just know the results of this leg.

My phone rings. It's Modesty. That's not her real name, she believes that her real name is boring, so she introduces herself as Modesty to people. I never knew what a real name was. I never knew what a boring name was. We were a couple, the two of us. She and Maroje were the only people I let read my stories. After she read them, she would always give me some criticism, and I'd always sulk. We arranged to meet each other.

I paid the coffee, for both me and Rale, and left.

*

Why?

It feels like I don't know you at all.

Don't you give me that.

You seem like someone out of a past life, Elias.

She didn't even notice that my shadow was missing.

I closed my eyes.

*

An ant was running in a circle, panicking. The puff of smoke I had sent its way completely bewildered it. Now I was chasing him around with my lit cigarette. This sadistic little game went on until I set the cigarette against my lips and took a drag. The sun leapt away, the shadows were becoming shorter, the windows flickered, the trams glided down tracks slick with last night's rain, and the people frantically clung to dreams that were fading away, trying to hold on to at least some sliver of them.

They never do, I thought; they wake up, and then they start their lives all over again. Their exhaustion reaches its peak on Friday, they sleep through Saturday, and then watch Formula One races on Sunday, all day, switching from channel to channel. The hours slip by, the boredom rises, and with it that terrible feeling of an impending Monday. I put out my cigarette—almost killing the ant in the process—and decided not to think about people and their routines.

I got up and rubbed my eyes. I didn't need a mirror, I knew my eyes were bloodshot and bleary. I walked by the tracks, followed by a shade, as silence and solitude walked behind it.

*

The sun snuck in through the blinds and outlined the dust motes flickering through the air. The heat, mixed with boredom, had taken its toll: I was lying in bed completely numb, trying not to move, not to breathe. My body was made of lead, and so were my dreams. The words that got stuck in my throat were made of lead as well, and so were the thoughts I couldn't complete.

When the light started to dim, when the afternoon shadows started to curiously peek out, I got up. Half-awake, I walked into the shower and let a stream of cold water wash over my body. The water broke down the lead, my thoughts finally started flowing, my limbs became lighter. My heart was beating again, and I was back in the realm of the living dead.

*

With my hair still wet, I sat on my balcony and drank coffee. It was a night of shadows, shadows moving like silhouettes over a photograph with double exposure. Everything was throbbing with life, and me? I was sitting alone, sipping cold coffee, swatting away mosquitoes. I grabbed my phone and called Maroje.

Hey, where are you?

Out on the town. What, you're up?

Seems so. Meet at the Mile? Half an hour?

Half an hour, you say? Sure.

Beep-beep-beep. I get up, put on my shirt, gather some change, and walk out. I look at the sky: the stars are spelling out words in some ancient language. A language of chaos. I don't speak it, but I can hear it. It's the language of the apocalypse. It's made out of silence.

I waited for the bus, snuck onto it through the back door and leaned back on my seat. Two girls, fourteen- or fifteen-year-olds, sat next to me. Alternative kids. Black sneakers, black clothes. One of them wore a shirt that was supposed to look Indian, but it was this season's model. Their purses were sprinkled with badges. From anarchy symbols and proclamations that *punk's not dead* all the way to peace signs. They wore their uniforms, fighting against corporate capitalism by force-feeding it money. A little way off stood a group of five or six boys, a bit younger than the girls. Polo shirts, baseball hats, white sneakers, and the vocabulary of sixteen-year-olds. They kept shouting remarks at the girls. I could see their near future—their vocabulary will stay the same, as will the number of books they've read, but their muscles will develop, and their voices will grow deeper. And they won't shout anymore. They'll just punch.

*

I felt the first rays of sunlight on my cheek. They weren't caressing me, they were teasing. The pillow was damp with saliva, and an entire side of my face was soaked from that same drool. A thought lingered in the back of my mind, one that would return every time I went overboard with alcohol the night before.

I'll never drink again.

The headache was, surprisingly, not there this time. I got up and wiped my cheek, instinctively taking a look at my watch, as if I had a meeting I was surely late for. I tried to remember the details of the previous night, but it was all more like a movie that I watched from a couch underwater. The characters were blurry and the sounds could barely reach me. I took a shower, made coffee, and sat on my balcony.

I thought you didn't like routine, a voice tells me. A girl. I turn around, and it's Modesty—I didn't notice when she came in.

I don't, it's just that . . .

. . . it's just that it's easy to give in to it. I know.

I have a feeling that we've already had this conversation.

So there's no need to repeat it?

None. Coffee?

She nodded. I went to get a cup and poured her some coffee.

Milk, no sugar?

She nodded again and I poured her some milk. We sat and drank without saying a word.

Elias, when was the last time you took a walk around town? She broke the silence without looking at me.

Yesterday, as a matter of fact.

No, a real walk. Not on your way to a club.

I tried to recall.

Would you like to go for a walk? She looked at me.

*

The night is soft.

I laughed. I didn't know what that meant.

Can't you feel it?

What?

The carefree emptiness of the city.

I see the emptiness of the city, if that's what you mean.

No, no. Can't you feel that the city air is different?

I don't know what you mean, I shrugged, but I can feel it's going to rain tonight.

How can you tell?

The smell of the asphalt.

We walked down Zrinjevac Square when the first drops of rain fell on the asphalt, darkening it. Soon it was pouring, and we took shelter under the gazebo in the middle of the square and watched the people running around, looking for cover, as umbrellas scattered all round us.

Modesty?

Yes?

I think I've stopped looking.

Come again?

I don't look at things anymore. I can see the sky through the branches of the tree, and that's all it is to me, a sky without the tree. I don't see it as I used to. It's the same with the faces of building, or clotheslines on balconies. There was a time when I could see a certain beauty in these things, a stanza, the opening line of a story. Lately all I can see is still frames.

She looked at me. She didn't say anything, she just went up to me, stood on her toes and kissed me on the cheek. The rain soon stopped, and we headed towards the train station.

Wrapped in a cloak of silence, we waited for the light to turn green. Modesty was checking her fingernails, and an old chorus rang in my head, something about traffic lights. A young couple with a child stood on the other side of the road. The kid couldn't have been older than five, and he twiddled a plastic gun in his hand. His parents were arguing over something and paid no mind to their young Clint Eastwood. The kid kept twirling the gun, faster and faster, until it finally slipped from his fingers and hit the pavement. The two of them glanced at the gun and continued their argument. The light turned green. As we walked past them, I told the Kid Eastwood:

Screw it, Kid, we'll never make a gunslinger out of you.

*

I opened my eyes.

And that was it? She gave you no other reason?

There were no fireworks, no confetti, if that's what you're asking. Not even a raised voice.

She just left?

Yes. In the course of the same day, both my girlfriend and my shadow left me.

Maroje ordered two more beers. Maroje and I are very much alike. We both think (erroneously, it would seem) that we're erudite on the subjects of literature and rock 'n roll. The important difference is that he doesn't get his fingers messy when he writes with a felt tip pen.

She's gone, turn to the next best thing.

And that would be?

He took a sip of beer. I wasn't sure if that really was the next best thing, but I did it anyway.

RED SHIFT

If it takes shit to make bliss,
I feel pretty blissfully
                    —Modest Mouse

This story starts with a cliché, a loser cliché. I was hungover, my girlfriend had left me, and my shadow had gone missing. Not all clichés are bad, and this one was a good picture of my mental state over the past three or four days. Idleness, self-pity and always a beer too many. I hadn't left my apartment for days. I had bought a dozen beer cans, two bottles of wine, and invited Maroje over to keep me company. I woke up, hungry and barely able to walk. I yawned, walked out of my room and into the world.

A look in the mirror reveals the face of a twerp who doesn't shave, sleeps too little, bites his lips, and doesn't comb his hair. Conclusion number one, the twerp doesn't take care of his appearance and isn't a shallow cunt like the rest of the population of this planet. Conclusion number two, conclusion number one is just an excuse for laziness and bad habits. Conclusion number three, the situation hasn't changed over the last year. I take a razor and a brush for shaving cream, and I run water over them. In swift moves I apply the shaving cream and shave myself. A look in the mirror reveals a shaved twerp who sleeps too little, bites his lips, and doesn't comb his hair.

The traffic lights change. The days become colder, and I start toying with the idea of finally leaving my apartment.

I eat cereal for breakfast. That's a trigger for another soppy flashback about my relationship with Modesty. It reminded me of the days when she would sit at the kitchen table for an hour, chain smoking and poring over a manuscript— my manuscript. Too many descriptions, she would say, needless virtuosity and useless streams of consciousness; also, your protagonist is too macho and some images repeat themselves. Her cornflakes would be soggy and completely inedible, her coffee would go cold. She was dressed in just her undershirt and panties, her bare feet would touch the cold kitchen tiles, and now and again she would curl up her toes or flick ashes off the manuscript. The morning sun shone its rays through the dim windowpane—dim because they hadn't been cleaned in months—and lit up the kitchen, while I sat in the living room, a pile of books scattered on the table in front of me, several notebooks stained with coffee, an empty bowl, and the TV screen. I twitch. My cornflakes have gotten too soggy from the milk. I give up on the idea of going outside.

I get into the bathtub. I don't know how much time I spent staring straight ahead into nothingness, but the water had gone cold and I was knocked down. Reality had caught me on the chin with an uppercut, and I could hear the referee counting down the seconds. I wouldn't get up; the flurry of blows would just have gone on. My cellphone rings from the pocket of my pants crumpled up next to the tub.

Hey, I heard Andrea dumped you.

Yeah, so have I.

You okay?

I've been sitting in my tub for over an hour.

Oh my.

Without my rubber ducky.

Oh my.

Yeah.

On my way.

That was Vanda. Vanda worried too much about me. Vanda was into photography. That whole conversation reminded me of a dialogue from *Franny and Zooey*. I stare at the stains on the ceiling. Their shapes are unclear. I submerge. The shapes are still unclear.

*

And that was it? She gave you no other reason? No fireworks, no confetti? No raised voices? She just left?

Yes.

Oh my.

I've lost my shadow.

It happens to every boy who doesn't want to grow up.

Why does everyone keep saying that?

She shrugged. A couple of moments of silence ensued.

It's the Doppler effect, I said.

What?

The Doppler effect. When you hear it approaching, like, a train for example. It keeps getting louder and louder, and then the noise reaches its peak, and then it gets gradually more quiet as it disappears into the distance.

Like Andrea?

Yes, like Modesty. I felt the noise peak just a while ago, and now it's growing quiet, more distant.

So it's a matter of time.

In a little while I won't even see her anymore. I might hear a dull echo from time to time, and that's it.

I pick up the paper and leaf through it. Vanda asks me what I need the paper for. I scan the classifieds. I have to find myself a new shadow.

WENDERS AND HOT CHOCOLATE

I feel as if I'm in a dream in the darkness of the movie theatre. Paralyzed I sit and stare at the colorful, shining pictures zipping across the screen, unable to look away and think of something else. I watch movies all by myself, and I dream with Modesty by my side, and it is then that my whole body trembles, full of life. I lean my head on her skinny shoulder and inhale the scent of body milk mixed with the scent of spring. That's her smell. She always sleeps in a huddle, which makes me cling to her tight, so I can catch all her nightmares and take them on for her. I love her so much that I often dream of her dying.

Waking up used to be nice. She would wake up before me, open the window, sit on the windowsill, and light the morning's first cigarette, which, she claims, tastes the best. Every cigarette tastes bad to me, and I don't actually understand why I smoke. And so, Modesty would smoke and watch the streets slowly fill up with people. Sometimes a person on the street would look up and see a skinny girl smoking on the windowsill, dressed in nothing but panties and an undershirt. Who knows what crossed their minds then. I would have thought she was a fallen angel, recovering from the previous night's party. As it was, I just woke up and watched her. Every day I discovered a new detail.

I start with her feet. Red nail polish on her toes. I follow the line of her leg up to her knees, scarred and bruised like a child's. The line reaches her panties and her bony hips. The leg closer to the window is completely stretched out, forming an almost perfect triangle with the other leg. Her body and head leaning against the frame of the window, she watches the street. One of her shoulder straps sometimes slips down. Her brown, unkempt hair flows under her chin, and her two obsidian stones, still half-asleep, note everything going on on the other side of the window. One of her arms hangs loose next to her body, and the other one is holding a cigarette. She usually had red fingernails, but this time the polish is a bit chipped.

I get up and kiss her. She flicks the cigarette out the window, comes down, stands on her toes and kisses me, and walks silently toward the kitchen. These silent mornings echoed the loudest in my memories.

*

Back in the movie theatre, once again. Frames of fantasy stream down the silver screen. A river of thoughts and memories. The worst kind of masochism. I catch myself in the middle of a street, staring into a puddle reflecting the lights and lives around me. A cigarette on my lips, but I've misplaced my lighter somewhere. I stand, frozen, unable to sync with the world. And suddenly everything stands still. The people, the trams, the sky, the rain, the hurt, the suicides. Can you imagine how those people feel, frozen in time while committing suicide? A static moment of death, an eternal wait for the fall.

I spin on my heel and look around. It really is true, nothing is moving, everything is defying the laws of physics. Except for me. Once again, I've been denied, bound by the laws of physics: Mother Nature and Father Time. And yet people are puzzled when I say that I'm a loser and the butt of jokes from gods current, retired, and forgotten.

I can hear footsteps. Ha! That means I'm not the only loser, there are more of us. Perhaps it's a young contender, set on seizing my title. Well, no dice! The only thing worse than being the biggest loser is being the second in line. But, what I saw was myself. It disturbed me, to say the least.

Do you see now, the other me says.

Do I see what? The only thing I see is my friendly face and a frozen city.

You've lost your shadow, and nothing seems to be going your way.

Things are going just fine.

So that's why you left the theatre before the end of the movie? I thought you liked Wenders.

I do. I just stepped out to . . .

Get some fresh air? Look, you can't fool me. You're fucked. You're out of ideas, you're out of work, you've lost your girl-friend, and you've even lost your lighter.

I don't want to have a job. I swore an oath not to. That, and that I'd never comb my hair.

He walks up to me, takes out a lighter and lights my cigarette.

Who are you? I ask him.

I'm your shadow.

Well, I'm no genius, but shadows tend to be black and grey, are usually found on floors and walls and don't talk.

How do you explain me, then?

I shrug my shoulders. He walks up to me, takes the ciga-rette from my mouth and flicks it away.

Drop the act. Stop smoking. You're twenty, act your age. If you have to be lost, be a lost boy, not a lost idiot.

Why is everyone around me using these Peter Pan metaphors?

It's definitely not because you're mature and give away the impression of a stable, formed personality.

I don't want my personality to be formed, that would mean there's no room to fit anything else in. And I'm not lost, because how can I get lost on the way if there's no rest waiting for me at the end of the journey?

That's the first smart thing I've heard from you. Write it down, start writing again, get a move on.

She was right. I need to get a move on, drag myself out of the mud, stop dreaming and line up the stars in my favor. I couldn't do it on my own. I needed my shadow.

How come you disappeared, man? Or . . . girl? What do I call you, since you're a shadow? A man-shadow? Shadowman?!?

Shadow is fine. You needed something that would make you stop pitying yourself.

Modesty leaving me wasn't enough?

You needed to realize that everything you needed was within you, not in anybody else.

I fell silent for a long while, and the Shadow snapped me out of my musings.

So, what was the movie like?

Fucked up. Instead of Wenders, I got some sort of retrospective. I tried to get my money back, but the guy at the counter wasn't too understanding.

Better luck next time, kiddo.

So, what now?

Go home, get some sleep. Beginning tomorrow, we start working on you.

I managed to hop on board a tram at the last minute. All the way home I stared out the window. A crescent moon hung in frozen sky, and some guy sat on its horn, reading a newspaper.

Maroje and Mislav are sitting at the kitchen table, debating some lofty topic, not paying much mind to me. I open the fridge and realize that the beer is gone. I ask about coffee. The coffee is gone as well, they've made hot chocolate.

Great, I say.

Of course, it's gone cold by now.

I don't mind.

I sit at the table, ashes and coffee stains everywhere. Maroje puts out his cigarette and asks me how the movie was. I send him the answer telepathically, but he doesn't get it. He says that Modesty called, I need to pick up my stuff from her place. I drink my chocolate and sprawl over the couch. I dream of a desert where the sand is the color of her skin, where nights are as dark and bright as her eyes.

HAPPY AND DEAD

That morning Andrej Kalovski found out that he was dead. He was breathing, his heart was still pounding, his whole body kept ticking without a hitch but, there was no way around it, he was dead. He drank his coffee, tying his tie with his free hand: that was a skill acquired over years of working in a grey company with grey hallways, where everyone wore grey suits, drank bland coffee, and ate free lunches that somehow tasted grey. In addition to tying his tie with one hand, Andrej had also learned to approach all spheres of his life with apathy. The realization that he was dead did not shock him in the slightest: he kept sipping his coffee, his tie already in place. On his way out of the apartment, his wife reminded him to take out the trash.

Stepping outside, he was greeted by the early morning cold and silence; there was almost nobody in the street. He headed to the bus stop, where he boarded his bus every day at 7:22 and went to work. He would see the same faces at the bus stop every morning, standing in the same spots. However, today he saw a new person. A short girl with black, messy hair. He could clearly see traces of mascara around her large black eyes, and fainter traces of bags under her eyes. Her black shirt was too large and her jeans too tight; she looked at him, smiling, as if they knew each other. He saw her lips move, but didn't hear what she was saying.

I'm sorry, I can't hear you.

I didn't say anything.

Oh. I thought . . .

I was just moving my lips.

I can't read lips.

I'll teach you. Try again.

Andrej watched her lips move again, carefully forming each muted syllable. Do-you-have-a-ci-ga-rette?

I don't.

There you go! See, it's not that hard. Besides, I don't smoke.

Then why do you want a cigarette, miss?

Drop the miss.

Excuse me?

Why. Do. You. Want. A. Cigarette., she replies.

Ah, okay. Why do you want a cigarette? he asks.

To strike up a conversation.

The bus arrives, Andrej gets on, and the girl stays at the bus stop.

Hey, aren't you coming?

No, it's crowded, I'll catch another one.

But . . .

Andrej spent the whole day thinking about her. While he was waiting for the bus with a co-worker, he looked at him. Do-you-have-a-ci-ga-rette?

Excuse me?

I didn't say anything, I was just moving my lips.

His co-worker looked at him, confused. Andrej, you've been working too hard.

Yeah, perhaps.

He came come. He had dinner. He didn't have sex with his wife. Before drifting off to sleep, he thought about the strange girl from the bus stop. Perhaps he'll see her in the morning.

Morning. He drank his coffee, tying his tie with his free

hand: a skill acquired over years of working in a grey company with grey hallways, where everyone wore grey suits, drank bland coffee, and ate free lunches that somehow tasted grey. On his way out of the apartment, his wife reminded him to take out the trash.

There she was! She was tying a shoelace while hopping on her free foot. The people at the bus stop paid her no mind.

Hello! He walked up to her.

She looked at him and kept tying the shoelace.

My co-workers can't read lips, either.

She ties her laces. She folds her arms across her chest and checks the bus schedule.

What's wrong, don't you remember? I'm the guy you asked for a cigarette yesterday, and you don't even smoke.

She remains silent. The bus arrives. He looks at her, boards and sits down, deflated. Yesterday must have been just a game for her. The doors close, and she jumps in at the last moment. She approaches him.

I dreamt that I was bungee-jumping to Earth from space.

What?

Yes. The feeling was amazing.

I mean, why didn't you talk to me at the bus stop?

I did, yesterday.

So?

But I didn't get on the bus with you.

I still don't get it.

That's how I achieve a feeling of completeness. I didn't talk to you at the stop, but I will on the bus. So there.

What about tomorrow?

What?

What will you do tomorrow?

What's tomorrow?

The day after today.

That's a bit of a fuzzy concept for me. I'm not able to see that far.

Oh. Bungee, you say?

Yes! The planet was getting closer and closer, and just a moment before impact, the rope pulled me back out again.

I never dream interesting things.

I don't believe you.

No, really. I only dream about exams, the worst ones, from college.

Make a change.

I don't know how to make changes in dreams.

You don't have to. Make some in your life.

What should I do?

Quit your job.

Yeah, right, should I leave my wife while I'm at it?

Why not? Do you love her?

What do you . . . of course I do!

You love her so much it rhymes, it seems. This is my stop, bye.

Andrej was left baffled. So baffled that he almost forgot to get off at his stop. Make a change. That sounds so nice. So magical and simple. But it also requires a lot of courage. On his way home from work, he looked for the girl. At the stop. On the bus. In other people. Next morning he asked her what her name was.

Megi.

That's your real name?

What's a real name?

What's the name on your ID card?

Why would a piece of plastic know my real name?

Well, how did your parents name you?

Why would *they* know my real name?

All right, I'll call you Megi. Hi, I'm Andrej.

He reached out and they shook hands.

Have you quit your job?

No.

I take it you're still married, then.

Yes.

So what changes have you made?

None.

You're a coward.

I know, but . . .

But, but, but, but! She covered her ears with her palms. Start with the little things, then. Squeeze out toothpaste from the middle of the tube.

How did you know I always started at the end?

I know everything. Angels and prophets whisper to me.

In your dreams?

No. In the street.

How come I don't see them?

You don't need to see them. It's enough to listen. This is my stop, bye! She runs out of the bus.

It was a foggy morning. He drank his coffee, tying his tie with his free hand: a skill acquired over years of working in a grey company with grey hallways, where everyone wore grey suits, drank bland coffee, and ate free lunches that somehow tasted grey. On his way out of the apartment, his wife reminded him to take out the trash.

Do you read? Megi asked him at the bus stop.

I read the papers.

The papers are much too heavy for me.

What do you mean?

All that news: the suffering, the frauds, the murders, the spectacle. It makes me sick.

What do you read?

Poetry.

What kind?

She shrugged. All kinds.

I haven't read poetry in a long time.

Come with me to a poetry reading tonight.

Where? And who's reading?

My friends are reading, at their place.

Does that qualify as a poetry reading?

Why wouldn't it?

Well, it's not official.

What does *official* mean? She laughed.

Okay, I get it. When?

Depends on when you get off work.

Around seven or eight.

Want me to meet you here at half past eight?

It's a deal.

The bus arrived. They got on and continued to talk. About autumn and the smell of chestnuts. About the morning fog. About the expanding universe. According to her. Andrej thinks it might compress in the end. A reverse Big Bang. At half past eight they meet at the bus stop. When he asked her if the apartment was far, she said it wasn't. After a five-minute walk, they reached the apartment.

The fourteenth floor. The apartment wasn't big. A single room and bathroom. Books and candles were everywhere, so Andrej had to be careful not to knock over a stack of books or a pile of vinyl LPs. Music was coming from a gramophone (well, actually, from a speaker, but they only explained that to him later). He didn't recognize the band because he never listened to music. Megi told him that they were called Gang of Four and that she thought they were a bit overrated. Megi's friends drank wine.

Sis, who's the fella? one of them asked. Tall, thin, dark-haired. He looked like he laughed a lot.

Andrej, he said, and held out his hand. The boy's name was Pavel. The other boy was called Yeshu. He was a bit shorter, had brown hair and green eyes.

Hana's late, per usual, Pavel spoke. But I think that we can begin.

Yeshu reaches out for an old book with yellowed pages. *I saw the best minds of my generation . . .* he starts reading.

You can't read Ginsberg every time, Pavel complains. Last time you read *Sunflower Sutra*.

Last time I read *America*.

Doesn't matter, it's always these Yanks with you, Megi butts in. The discussion goes on, various names are mentioned, and Andrej listens to them, lost in the names. Someone rings the doorbell.

It's Hana, Yeshu says. Hana is a tall, dark-haired girl. She announces that she has started writing a new poem.

Let's hear it, Pavel says, pouring more wine for himself.
Sometimes
in the middle of automated actions
I stop
and look around
as if saying to myself
it's all right
as if saying to myself
everything will be okay
you're still here
you're still around something in me is still capable of
changing my direction
once, when you're gone
you won't even know it

          or wonder

             or look around

That's true, Andrej speaks for the first time. Nothing changes my direction. I never look around. I fit in seamlessly into the machine. I didn't even require oiling. And the more I talk to Megi, the clearer I see that there are choices, that choices can scare a person, and that's why it's easiest to walk down well-trodden paths.

Silence ensued. The record was over, a soft hum was coming out of the speakers, and Pavel took another sip of wine. You know, he started, your situation is not as bad as you think. There are people who never realize this. And there are people who spend their entire lives thinking that they're free, and end up being slaves to such insignificant things. In the end, everything you need is already within you. That's the part that's hard to understand. I've known that sentence for years, and I still don't get it completely. A friend once dreamt that people were being swallowed by a gluttonous god of mediocrity. And some of these people had ideas, wanted to change the world, but they had sold out the present for a safe past. They started a frenzied race against time. And all these people, they were happy. Happy and dead.

A moth circles frantically around the flame of a candle, and finally rushes through it. It doesn't die, doesn't drop to the floor twitching its legs. It keeps circling round, its wings on fire. It burns. It blazes. Megi opens the window and the moth disappears down the throat of the night, turning into an orange dot. For a moment, it looks like it might set the night on fire.

THROW AWAY YOUR CELLPHONE

I dreamed of snow, I told her. The sky was purple, and everything around me was grey and white. It was snowing, and that was the only sound I could hear.

She doesn't say anything and blows out a bluish ring of smoke. It turns into a thousand tiny serpents which disappear just a moment later.

Yesterday I dreamed of the last moments of the world, I continued. The sky was barren, the stars were going out in blazing supernovas. Everything was racing back to the beginning, and I was unusually calm.

Every night is the same. The same people are always drunk, the same trams are always late. Neon lights glimmer on wet sidewalks, the rain falls silently and the whole town goes silent. The taxis glide down the streets, their engines quietly humming, and moths circle the streetlights frantically. The city is an orchestra playing a lullaby.

Every night is the same, and all the characters we see through the smoke of our joints are always the same. Repeating visions, blue silhouettes. Every beer spins our world in the same way. Every night is the same, and the ensuing hangover is always equally nauseating. And there's nothing new under the heavens or the neon.

A light was on in the room, its orange glow outlining the furniture. Through the half-closed shutters we could see the buildings and the night, and the sky the color of a ripe cherry. We were silent, so the only noise was soft jazz coming from the stereo. The best thing about jazz is that you can listen to it, leave the room for two or three minutes, and come back feeling like you haven't missed anything. The melodies and rhythms flow like a river, and you can relax, knowing for sure that it won't strand you on the rocks.

We stayed silent while everything around us was still. The jazz went quiet and our thoughts froze. The color of the morning sky was shifting from red into azure, and what had been shadows and outlines were now grey concrete blocks merging with the sky. I closed my eyes. When I opened them again, I was alone in the apartment, and I didn't know what time it was. I got up and stretched.

Okay, I say, let's grab a bite. I walk to the fridge and open it. Milk, some kind of juice, and a lot of stuff that I'd need to cook or fry first. Eggs will do fine. I eat, listen to the radio, and think. Man, she's gone, and didn't even bother to leave a note. Oh well, eat, shower and then head home.

Under the shower I thought of a good opening sentence for a story, but it followed the water down the drain. A lot of good ideas emerge under the shower. I sip my coffee and wait for my hair to dry. I try to remember the sentence that's lost in the waterways underneath the city. I realized that it's impossible to be alone these days. It's as if something is always interrupting us; the ringing of phones, cellphones, always something, *immer etwas*. The noise and other people's problems are our faithful companions.

My cellphone rang. I didn't even look to see who was calling. I threw it out the window. Throw away your cellphone, time to make this clean decision. Bye-bye, noise, bye-bye, other people's problems. I went out into the street and breathed in the autumn air. Chestnuts, firecrackers, and rotting leaves. The passersby looked up. Some maniac had thrown his cellphone out the window. I saw its remains. There was no one to mourn it. Bye-bye, common sense. I stuffed my hands down my pockets, let myself miss the tram and started walking home. The sun finally shone, after a hundred years of darkness. But darkness is a matter of perspective, because colors are everywhere. The colors are inside us, and we shine like neon lights; that's how the lyrics to that song went. Autumn's nervous strokes splattered the streets in yellows and reds. The city was a Pollock. I peered at the sun, grinning like an idiot, as my shadow danced across the windows.

God, what a day.

What kind of day? my Shadow asked me.

A day to make decisions. Good decisions.

Whatever you say. By the way, that was Modesty back then, calling your cellphone.

Elias, your timing really is terrible, I tell myself. Oh well, what can you do? I kept walking down the street, a slight jig in my step, whistling one of Serge Gainsbourg's songs. People stared at me, puzzled. It was obvious that they hadn't seen anyone in a good mood for a while. The coat of madness I was wearing fit me well.

*

Hello, Elias, it's Modesty (Yes, I know who it is). I know we haven't talked in a long while (A year, two? At least it seems that way), but I think that enough time has passed and that we can talk again. She fell silent, and I imagined her biting her lower lip, thinking about how to continue. I have a lot of questions. What have you been doing? Where have you been?

No, actually, don't answer that. Get in touch when you hear this message, I think we should meet.

A beep, and then silence. A whole eternity had passed. The apocalypse and a new creation of the universe, the grand circle of things. A whole eternity had passed, and I thought: that damn girl.

*

I could clearly see her lipstick on the cigarette butt. Some kind of leaden fog had descended on my mind, and I knew the pill was kicking in. She took me by the hand, got up and headed to the bedroom. A thousand thoughts raced through my head, and I couldn't grasp any of them. Her lips against mine, her fingers digging into my back, tracing maps that, when I see them in the mirror, take me back to a room that existed only in that moment. With a kiss she drained all the thoughts from my head, and all that was left was instinct, and there really was nothing at all around us.

*

The smell of her perfume, mingled with my day-old Old Spice, had crept into the pillow. For a while I just lay there, breathing the smell as the memories of the night before glided before my closed eyes, brushing against my eyelashes. She was in the bathroom, talking to me about something. I didn't hear her.

Sorry?

I said: you've built a bridge between you and the world, it's longer than the Golden Gate. I can't see where it ends, she said, putting on lipstick.

I can't see any bridge. That bridge metaphor is far-fetched,

I can be close to people. It's not like I detest the dust of the world.

I think my hips are too big, I've realized that by looking at my shadow, she says, and goes back to putting on lipstick.

I get out of bed and put on my pants. She's already all dressed up. There are flowers in the hallway, the same color as her lipstick. I look at her.

Since when do you care about your appearance?

I need to go. I'll call you later. She kisses me on the cheek, opens the door, and the darkness of the hallway swallows her.

Elias, how long will you keep doing this? Skipping from stone to stone, looking for faults in girls, and when you don't find any, or when they are so tiny and insignificant, you set your sights on another girl. And what's so different about her? You don't know her, she's a mystery, something new and, most importantly, she's not "yours." She's wrapped up in a coat made out of shadows, and her perfume smells like a happy ending. And in the end, you strip that coat off her, and what then, you twerp? You discover a bunch of flaws, and every one of them bothers you, but every one of them is tolerable. The girl still smells like a happy ending, but you're the one who screws things up.

And what's going on with Modesty? It's been so long, and you feel something that isn't there. You're trying to remember what it was like two, three years ago, or whenever. You're trying to recreate that feeling. You take out the photo album, look at the Polaroid pictures. And nothing. But you're still convinced you'll have a happy ending with her.

Am I? I'm not so sure anymore. In fact, I know I'm not. And why am I here? I shudder, get a Post-it, take a felt tip pen out of my pocket and write a note, and stick it on her fridge. This is pointless. You look like someone from a past life. Goodbye. I get dressed and leave. The sun reflected on the snow, and I counted all the hues of white.

*

If I could write down all your dreams, I'm sure it would be the most beautiful book in the world, but I wouldn't want to share it with anyone.

*

It's been a couple of days, and I still don't want to leave my bed. The TV is on just so I can pretend I have some company. I've been thinking about all my failures, all my mistakes, all those harsh words. I think nothing hurt me more than when Marina V. wouldn't say hi to me anymore in elementary school. Marina was my kindergarten sweetheart.

I got up and typed her name into Facebook. She's not so pretty anymore, and she listens to turbofolk music. That's one wound less to worry about. I got back into bed and pulled my blanket up to my nose. On the TV, some guy just shot another guy over a woman.

*

My second biggest disappointment (the first was Marina V.) was when I realized that archaeology had nothing to do with beating up Nazis, Atlantis, or lost artifacts. Goddamn Hollywood.

*

At night, on my way home across the marketplace, I would sometimes run into a tiny old lady with big eyes, who would hold out her hand and ask me for a couple Kuna. Every time, I would ignore her and walk by. My conscience would start nagging me, and sometimes I felt so bad I cried. In the morning I'd feel bad.

That day I felt worse than ever. Not because I'd turned my head away from the old lady, or because I'd read the papers and once again realized that it's a cruel, wicked world. I felt worse than ever because of that damned girl. And I had a dream. I dreamed about snow and the end of the world, and the static on the TV screen. When I opened my eyes again, a thousand lifetimes had passed, and I was still alone, while the glow of the streetlights shone through the blinds. I reached out towards the switch and flicked on the light. I frowned as my eyes adjusted to the electric glare of the lamp.

I put on my hoodie and jacket, and decided to go for a walk, maybe get some cigarettes. The streets outside were completely empty. I walked at an easy pace, watching the shadows of the skyscrapers and the bright purple sky. I was a shadow, and the world around me seemed eerie. I soon saw the sign CORNER 0-24.

There was just one man at the kiosk. When I got closer, I realized that it was an older man, dressed as an old-school Burgher, with a top hat on his head. He gave me a look. I looked away and asked the guy in the kiosk for some cigarettes. I paid him and turned to the old man. He was still looking at me, with a peaceful smile on his face, like a statue of Buddha covered in birdshit.

Hello, he said.

Good morning, I replied.

PICTURE POSTCARDS FROM
TRAIN STATIONS

One ought to be rich
and travel
and check the truth behind those postcards
          —Zvonko Karanović

As to the truth behind the following stories, or memories, don't bet your life on it. The past is a tricky thing, and the catch is that nobody remembers what really happened. We add colors, movie moments. It's something like Photoshop.

Let's say that I'm holding a photo album. This gives me authenticity as the storyteller, and besides, a photo album is much more poetic than scrolling through pictures on your computer or smartphone. The past becomes tangible. Photographs are subject to the laws of physics. See, this is also how I confirm my theory about our skewed recollections of everything that happens.

The first photo was taken at the Münster train station. Stephan, my teacher, and I are sitting on a bench and waiting for the train to come. He's rolling a cigarette, and I'm reading Rilke or Fauser, I can't remember anymore. The picture was taken by Rafi.

*

MUNSTER—ENSCHEDE

Jean, or whatever the Frenchman's name was, was tuning his guitar. Stephan was already in his position at the electric drums, a joint in his mouth and a grin on his face. The Rastaman in charge of the bongos was just grinning like an idiot. Rafi the Afghan (I guess that was his nickname) was rummaging through a bunch of papers. Poetry. His. It was kinda okay. He was, it seemed, going to sing. And where was I in this picture? In the corner of the room, a bass guitar in my hands, slung low, just like Paul Simonon, or that dude from Interpol.

At first glance, the room seemed to belong to a student, and not a thirty-something Afghan guy. The lights were turned down low, books were scattered around, and the room was brimming with various records and CDs, cigarette butts and makeshift ashtrays, and dodgy company. Rafi had chosen the path of poetry, living on the expense of the state and his brother. It suited him just fine. I played the first couple of notes.

Nicht so laut, not so loud, said Stephan, the joint still between his lips. *Die Nachbaren sind Spiesser.* He said that the neighbors were square and that they would call the cops. I laugh and start playing "Guns of Brixton." Everybody bursts out laughing, except Jean, or whatever his name was.

Good bass line, he said. Is it yours?

No, no. I answer in English. It's by a band called The Clash.

Never heard of them.

Never heard of them? Man, they're the best band of all time.

I only know classical music, and some flamenco.

It's all rock 'n' roll, Stephan said. He picked up a beat,

cheerful, fast. I started playing along to it. It sounded like ska. Jean, or whatever his name was, got it pretty soon, and the Rasta gently played along. I don't know whether it was because we were high, or because music can take you to higher spheres, into the Empyrean, that final, immovable heaven, but several hours passed since we'd started playing. I felt like it had been ten minutes. Everyone had fallen asleep except Stephan, Rafi, and myself.

Something came over us and we decided, wonderfully high as we were, to take a ride around town in Stephan's car. Sunlight was faster than usual that morning. We sat in the car, put on shades, played some Oasis, and swerved down the streets. I rolled a joint, highly inexpertly, and handed it to Rafi.

This is the life, he said.

What is? Driving around and getting high? Doesn't seem like much, really.

No, not that, but the three of us. Not giving a damn about anything else.

I'm not sure that's so great either. Apathy kills, they say.

You're just a pessimist.

I shrugged and fell silent. All three of us did. We were out of pot.

Let's go get some more, Stephan suggested.

Good idea. Call your dealer.

No, let's go to Holland.

In this state? I asked. Man, there's no way they'd let us cross the border like this.

We'll take the train.

And so we found ourselves at the Munster Bahnhof, still high as kites. We bought tickets to the nearest Dutch town. It was Enschede.

I read somewhere that we remember in our dreams, I tell

Stephan. The landscape on the other side of the glass is blurry, dissolved. Rafi is asleep, awkwardly folded over himself in his seat.

Remember what?

I don't know. Anyway, does it matter? We're obviously sorely lacking something. How would you explain progress if it weren't so?

The only thing I can tell you about Enschede is that the grey sky there started an inch above the rooftops and that the local soccer club sucks. I can't remember anything else about it. We bought some weed, took a walk, grabbed a bite to eat in a fast food joint, and went back. When I think back on it, that wasn't the smartest decision. Stephan could have gotten away with being caught with the weed. Rafi and I would have been fucked. An Afghan and a guy from the Balkans would mean just one thing to a Western mind: bloodshed. And so the attendant in the train eyed us suspiciously, and the seconds ground to a halt.

Drogenturisten, he waved us off. That was the only thing that could be said about us. Just three guys, blasted out of their skulls.

*

The shattered glass lit our way, and every shard of it was a Razor Moon on this frozen night. Soon we heard the basses, shaking our bodies in waves, drowning out our conversation, straining our vocal cords. The brick walls were covered with posters and stickers and the entire alley reeked of piss. A bouncer stood in front of the entrance to the club, but he was way too thin and short. Definitely too thin to toss Rudiger out, and definitely too short to toss me out. We decided to finish our cigarettes before we entered. I inspected the bouncer, and almost felt sorry for him. I say *almost* because a couple of days earlier one of his colleagues roughed me up when I'd tried to sneak a beer into the club. The poor bastard was standing outside, and it was probably the coldest night in the past couple of months. The door opened, a young girl stepped out to talk on her cellphone, and we could hear "Crying Lightning" by the Arctic Monkeys playing inside.

Immer die selbe, scheiße Musik, Rudiger grumbled.

I shrugged. Still beats the Beatles.

A pimply-faced teenager with effeminate bangs and sickly eyes approached us. He tried to bum a cigarette.

Verpiss dich, Rudiger tells him without so much as a glance. I give the kid a cigarette anyway.

Of course, and when you run out of them, you'll just ask me for some. He flicked his cigarette to the ground as the kid walked away. Let's go inside. My balls have crept up into my body from this cold.

Shouldn't we wait for Luis?

He waves me off. That asshole is always late, no point in waiting for him.

Every twitch of those mesmerized bodies made the air heavier and heavier, the music still unbearable, smoke licking our eyes wide open, wickedly venomous amphetamine stares stabbing through the air, and there was no point in drinking the beer because it got warm so quickly. So Rudiger switched to lemon vodka, and I stuck to whiskey with a drop of water. The girls weren't winking at me that night. All the better, because that would have led to a conversation, which meant running my throat ragged trying to yell louder than Dave Grohl's overproduced voice—or stepping outside and exposing myself to the frost, the Razor Moon and the uncaring

night. I lifted my eyes from the bottom of my glass and realized I'd lost Rudiger. Among the crowd I spotted a high brow
and a thick beard. I concluded it had to be Luis. I didn't wave;
it wouldn't have made a difference in that crowd. I went to get
another drink.

The bartender was busy giving free drinks to a bronzed
German broad whose tits were in imminent danger of spilling
all over the bar.

Junge! I shouted. The bartender motioned me to wait. I
cursed under my breath and shouted again. He rolled his eyes
and came up to me. I ordered a whiskey, this time a double,
so I wouldn't have to jostle my way through the crowd again,
I felt someone's hand on my shoulder. I turned around to see
Luis smiling at me. He started telling me something.

What? I yelled. I can't hear a word you're saying.

Look at Rudi, he pointed. Rudiger was boring three girls
in the corner of the club.

I wink at Luis and start walking to the corner, trying not
to spill my whiskey. I'm going to try to cockblock Rudi. The
girls are tall, wearing high heels, their red toenails poking out.
How the hell are they not cold? I approach Rudi from behind
and start singing in his ear.

A message to you, Rudy.

Verpiss dich.

I sling my arm around his shoulder and take a sip. I ignore
the girls. Rudi, you do realize you can't have all three of them?

He can't have any of us, one of them says. Bangs, short
brown hair, an obviously artificial color. A tight dress without
shoulder straps.

Why not? I ask.

They've got boyfriends, Rudiger says.

Luis comes over, taps me on the shoulder. I drink my

whiskey and motion for Luis to wait. You know, Rudi, that can't be the only reason they want nothing to do with you. If you think that these girls can only defend themselves from idiots like you by having a boyfriend—or pretending to have one—then you're a bit of a chauvinist.

How come you're so socially aware all of a sudden?

I just think that the fact that these girls are not in the company of their boyfriends doesn't automatically mean they want your company. Or anyone else's, for that matter. *Komm, lass uns gehen.* I pull Rudi away, turn around and I'm suddenly facing three burly guys who are obviously on the warpath. I realize Luis has vanished.

They obviously weren't lying when they said they had boyfriends, I tell Rudi. Hey guys, I say to them. We didn't mean anything by it, we didn't know they were with you.

Fuck 'em, Rudi says. Let's find some other sluts.

I closed my eyes. Why did he have to say that? Rudi suffered from an inferiority complex because, up until he was around seventeen, he had been a zit-faced little midget. Now he was the quintessential *Ubermensch.* He was also mildly chauvinistic. He never read any female authors, he faked being in love and was generally always looking to stir trouble. I opened my eyes. I heard snippets of phrases like "let's take this outside." Suddenly, one of the three burly guys pulls a knife on us, Rudi smashes a bottle against his head and he goes limp, falling on the floor; the crowd starts parting away from us instead of preventing further bloodshed, and I freeze up, strategically, and a blinding pain stings me under my left eye, making me stumble. I feel someone's soft hands grabbing hold of me as the girls scream at us to stop; I lift my gaze and see Rudi pressing one of the guys against the wall and beating on him relentlessly; some people intervene and pull the guy who blitzed

me away from me. I blink a couple of times to chase away
the spots buzzing before my eyes, and see that the bouncers
have Rudiger pinned to the floor and are kicking the shit out
of him. I realize that one of the girls, the one with the bangs,
caught me and broke my fall. I run towards Rudiger, but one
of the bouncers stops me.

Where do you think you're going?

Don't beat him. We'll leave.

Fuck off, kid.

I tried to get past him, but he grabbed me by the collar and
pushed me away. I stumbled and fell face first on the floor,
looking at three pairs of high heels. The same girl helped me
up again. I realized I was still holding a glass in my hand. A
broken glass. Blood was streaming down my palm. The girl
with the bangs took me by my other hand and led me to the
toilet. Rudiger got thrown out of the club. Or at least they
stopped beating on him. She sat me down on a toilet seat in
the ladies' room.

I need to get out, I tell her.

I need to patch you together first. You can't bleed out on me.

It's just a flesh wound.

You've watched too much *Monty Python*.

Wow, now you've risen in my opinion.

Are you sure it's not just because of the high heels?

How are your toes not freezing?

We came here by cab.

Oh.

She cleans my wound with a Kleenex. I'm not sure that's
such a good idea. I'm slightly disoriented and I observe her.
She lifts her eyes from my wounds and smiles. What are you
so confused about?

I'm not sure if it's because of the concussion or because of
the booze, but you look really pretty.

What a charmer, she says, taking a Band-Aid from her purse. I never did understand women's purses. She applies a Band-Aid to my palm. Now you have a new line on your hand.

What does it mean?

I don't know, I'm no expert at reading the stars.

The moon is as sharp as a razor.

What?

I've cut myself on the moon.

What?

Kiss me.

Don't push your luck.

If one of those apes is your boyfriend, you're pushing your luck.

They were drunk, and your friend provoked them.

Rudiger's not my friend.

What is he, then?

I'm staying at his place so I don't freeze to death in my dorm. They still haven't fixed the heating.

Oh.

Thank you.

You're welcome.

I'm Elias.

That's a pretty name. You're not from around here.

No.

Where are you from?

Croatia. What's your name?

Emma.

That's a pretty name. *Ich danke dir, Emmalein.* Can I kiss you anyway?

No.

That's okay too. I'll go get Rudiger. I take a lot of toilet paper, Rudi will need it.

Bye, Elias.

Bye. Be careful not to trip in those heels.

I go out. The amphetamine stares are no longer venomous; they've become mocking and curious. The left side of my face still hurts. Bound to leave a bruise. I walk out and see Rudi, sitting down and leaning against the wall across the street. He's smoking, and blood is dripping from his lips and cheeks. His temple and his lower lip are busted open. I crouch next to him and hand him some toilet paper.

Clean yourself up.

Fuck off.

You're an idiot. Did you have to provoke them?

They can fuck off as well. Where's that Spanish faggot?

He vanished before all hell broke loose. Smart guy. I get up and reach out my hand to Rudi. Come on, stop your fooling around.

I hate that song. He takes my hand and I pull him up. Where are we headed? he asks me.

Away from the Razor Moon, into the morning gray.

*

Pour me some more. I pass her my glass. Trembling, awkward hands. The words get snagged on my teeth. Marcela pours me a tequila, spilling some. Real Mexican tequila. Hits you right to your bones. She brought it from her home. I forgot the name of the town. She told me I was weak. I've gotten drunk from just three glasses of the stuff. I ask her for some Sprite to water this shit down.

No can do. Drink beer if you want something milder. Marcela isn't the most normal of creatures. Fake red hair, short, with the body of a dancer and the teeth of a hare. Eyes the color of dark coffee. Tanned. Nice skin. She smells like some flower with an exotic name that Lorca or some similar poet must have extolled in the context of death and the night. Her parents sent her to study in Europe. She lived in Berlin at first. Her parents realized that the apple of their eye was spending too much time partying, so they sent her to a smaller town, so she can finally finish her studies. She always complained about that. She drank and smoked a lot. She laughed loud, talked loud, and was loud in bed.

Drink up, she orders. I do. It burns. My stomach's in turmoil. I close my eyes. I can feel the ceiling lamp. It looks like the moon. It's the only light in the room. The moonlight is hot and it burns away on my skin. I'm sitting on a mattress, leaning against the wall. I get up, walk to the toilet. I vomit into it.

You're such a stud, my shadow teases me.

Stop, you know that I can't handle tequila.

Why drink if you can't hold your liquor?

Just shut up, please. I get up. I squeeze toothpaste into my mouth. I rinse it. I go back to her room.

Who were you talking to over there? She laughs at me.

To my shadow.

Your shadow?

Yes.

Who are you, Peter Pan?

His shadow can't talk, you idiot.

She leans in towards me and pushes me onto the mattress. I lie down. She sits on me. You're tired, she says. I'm horny, I tell her. She laughs. The moonlight is burning on her back. It is hot. She takes off her shirt. Small breasts. Compact. They fit right in my hand. They should be advertised on TV. We kiss. She squeals; she moans. No music, no fucking jazz, could ever sound better than the sounds of a girl's pleasure. It's the closest to the sound a newborn baby makes, it's so primal. Why, then, do the French call orgasm a little death? The French are a morbid nation, and yet they claim to know everything about love.

*

Why do you dye your hair? I'm still in bed. My hands are behind my head. I inspect the cracks in the ceiling.

It's easier to change the color of your hair than something important. It is easier to change your surroundings, skip town. It's important that the stage setting isn't always the same.

For me, the important thing was to go to a place where people speak a different language. Where they have different habits. A different rhythm.

But you still know the language. You understand what they're saying. Beneath every sky, people talk about the same things.

So why are you looking for things in different cities?

It's hard to stand in place. It's easier to give in to the illusion that the promised land is somewhere outside. That exactly the thing we need is waiting for us somewhere else.

When everything is already within us?

Everything is within us.

That's great. That means I don't have to get out of this bed.

Tell me, do you believe in destiny?

Nope. Destiny, that's supposed to mean being in the right place at the right time, and knowing all the correct answers and having the shoes to match, as well. Who could bear that level of Hollywood bullshit?

I'm off to college.

I'm not. I'll stay in bed.

Why?

You said it yourself. Everything is within us. I guess I'll find whatever I'm missing right here.

If you find out what it is, let me know.

Deal.

She gets dressed. I watch her shower in the morning sunshine. She puts on her clothes. I smell the scent of freshly made coffee. She kisses me. She smells of coffee, morning hygiene, and some exotic flower.

*

The display windows are glittering, the sky twitches like a TV set with a dodgy signal, poked by the spires of churches and cathedrals. The scent of cinnamon and Coca-Cola commercials, the town has turned into a Christmas county fair. I was seven or eight when I last felt the Christmas cheer, when my grandmother came to visit, by train, from this very town. She had brought along some presents for her grandchildren. Santa had nothing on Grandma. That asshole never gave me anything in person. The snowflakes drift down and melt on my coat and my hair. I watch them vanish in Marcela's hair. We walk together. We don't hold hands. That's what lovebirds do. We were best with what we had.

So, you're off to Me-ji-co tomorrow?

And you're off to Yugoslavia?

Something like that.

You won't buy me a present for Christmas?

I don't believe in Christmas.

Neither do I, but I believe in presents.

All right, I might get you something, but only if you bring more tequila from Mexico. I don't know how I'll live through next semester without it.

Oh, look, mulled wine.

We got some mulled wine, leaned against a wall, heating our hands on the cups in silence, cautiously sipping our drinks.

Will you tell your girlfriend?

Tell her what?

About us?

What is there to tell?

You're right. I won't tell either.

You have a boyfriend?

No, I just won't tell anyone. You'll probably brag to your friends that you had sex with a Mexican girl.

Perhaps.

Let's go to my place.

Let's.

The next morning I woke up before she did. No hangover. A blessing of tequila. It has something to do with chemistry. Hard liquor doesn't leave a hangover. I made some coffee and sat at the table. I wouldn't wait for her to wake up. I scribbled on a Post-it. I left her a nice little note.

To Marcela for Christmas. It was a good time. All the best,

E.

P.S. You're out of coffee, sorry.

STAVANGER

The photo was taken on some rocks over an endless, shimmering sea. Kristian, Sven, and I are standing there, wrapped in towers, our hair wet, peering into the camera. A girl took the photo. A German girl of Portuguese descent whose name I've forgotten.

For a couple of moments, I felt nothing. A couple of moments of pure oblivion. As if I was only just going to be born. I opened my eyes. Through the ocean green I see the sun and other slumbering bodies around me. And suddenly the full force of the Northern Sea pulls me back into life. It was like a fast-forward video, from my birth all the way to this moment. This moment, when the cold pierced me like icy bullets, when there was no sound, while others around me were also just waking up, newborn and thrust violently into life. It was the farthest point from the sun.

I break the surface, swallowing air. I watch as the other bodies emerge around me. I climb up the rocks. I somehow manage to cut my hand. The sunlight heats us up there, it almost pierces our bodies. I glance at the sailboats bobbing lazily, tied to the pier. We will move on shortly. As soon as we dry up. I picture us looting and pillaging villages, like Vikings. We probably will, too. Head straight to the first bar, down a couple of beers, snatch some Norwegian wenches, see what happens. It was the perfect plan.

SOME CITY BY THE SEA

In the photo, Andrea and I are laying out the table for lunch. A plastic table, plastic chairs, her head tilted up in front of the camera when it clicked, me hunched over, placing a plate on the table. Sven took the photo.

Sven and I are on the roof of Andrea's house. We don't count the stars, no way. We leave that to the lovebirds. We count our failures; there's many more of those, it seems. We talk about

politics-music-movies, Zen, Hawking, and black holes. He
lights up a joint. That's a ritual of ours. We wait for Andrea
and her girlfriends to go to sleep, then we head to the roof and
light up. They didn't like it. It'll make you dull, they'd tell us.
We didn't know how else to spend our time. A small town. No
clubs. A couple of shops, a beach, fat German tourists and two
grinning guys. More blessed than the Buddha.

I love her skin.

Cool.

Especially when it tastes of salt.

Cool. Her friends are stuck-up.

No, you just don't have any style.

You trying to say I dress badly?

Style's got nothing to do with that. Style pertains to a
higher tier.

I don't think that the word "tier" can be used in this context.

Doesn't matter. Style is something higher. An attitude. A
feeling.

Oh, really?

You just don't know the right answers.

Tell me, then. What are they?

I can't. That would be worse than cheating on a test.

You cheated on every single test in high school, you jerk.

Yeah, but it was okay. I have style.

                    *

You've been smoking again, Andrea says as she washes the
dishes.

Yes.

Fucking pot will make you dull.

That way of thinking will make you dull. In fact, it already has.

Excuse me?

Everything needs to be by the book. For fuck's sake, you go to bed at eleven.

Well, somebody needs to go to the store in the morning, and you slackers sleep until one in the afternoon.

I shrugged. Whatever.

You always say that.

No worries.

Or that.

Well, what do you want to hear?

I just don't want to fight.

Then stop inspecting me for defects and we might get somewhere.

Why can't we be like other couples?

What, fat and boring? No thanks. Besides, Shakespeare himself said that the course of true love never did go smooth.

Then our love is the truest. She kisses me.

After the kiss, I keep my eyes closed for a long, long time. Yeah, okay, if only I could be sure that it's love, and not apathy.

*

I watch these postcards and random photos. They don't manage to elicit nostalgia. Fuck it. I need moments, not hours, years and distorted memories.

MICHAEL JORDAN, MY GURU

Through speech we seek azure mornings
— Idoli

A makeshift ashtray looks like a bizarre sculpture by a contemporary artist. A bunch of cigarette butts sloshing in Coke at the bottom of a sawed-through plastic bottle, riddled with burn marks. The cigarette butts float on the surface like dead fish. Maroje stares at the sculpture, his masterwork.

Don't try to count the cigarettes, it'll just bum you out.

The vinyl record has been crackling for a while, and no one seems to have the energy to flip it to its B-side. In fact, only Maroje and I are still awake. Sven and Marin have been sleeping on the couch for hours now. Maroje and I had a drunken discussion about literature; it's becoming a habit of ours. I get up and walk to the bathroom. The bleary red eyes are fragments of the mosaic of last night's madness. In a drunken haze, we proclaimed that Nick Cave was God. We proclaimed that Cohen's "Hallelujah" was the most beautiful song in the cosmos and that a divine intervention must have occurred when it was being written. We were on the verge of tears while thinking about what could have happened if Mick Jones and Joe Strummer had met in 2001 and decided to get The Clash back together and make another album. We are both twenty-one and it seems that there's nothing else to life than music and pretty girls. Literature was useful only as a source of quotes for our attempts at seduction. We are both twenty-one and surrounded by miracles.

Hangovers are not among those miracles.

I dreamt about Michael Jordan and Scotty Pippen, I yell to Maroje.

What did they tell you?

Michael told me not to waste time on soccer if I'm good at basketball. I'm sure that there's a deeper meaning hidden somewhere in there.

You haven't spoken of Modesty in a long while.

Andrea.

She didn't like to be called . . .

By her regular name. Yes, yes. I know.

How come?

What is there to speak of? The fact that our paths crossed, that whole relationship, was nothing more than a glitch in the system, a mistake of the bureaucracy of fate.

Are you sure that this is not the resentment talking?

I'm not mature enough to be resentful.

True. Are you going home?

I nod. Call you later.

I walk outside into a sunny winter morning. I catch a tram. I put on my shades to ward off stimuli from my eyes. In fact, I go so far as to isolate myself completely from external stimuli. My thoughts are becoming too loud.

I've decided to step away from words and into silence. Words are like cement. When they pile up a couple of adjectives next to your name, they create a new identity for you. Something that's got nothing to do with you. Then you're done.

I get out of the tram. I walk past a schoolyard. The kids are playing football, the cranes on the edges of the neighborhood are clawing at the clouds, and the sparrows are washing themselves in a puddle. They're having a blast. I love puddles, they reflect the sky. Sometimes I stop and stare at my reflection in puddles, contemplating whether I'm real, or just a reflection of the guy in the puddle. If I'm a reflection, I'll disappear as soon as he moves. I stand and stare. It's okay, I'm still capable of stopping and wondering at the world around me. I enter the apartment and decide not to move for the rest of the day.

*

Jura was observing me from the corner of the room. He was the only one who didn't mind the dust. Jura is a spider. My friends told me that my room is a reflection of my mental state. I wasn't aware that a human soul can become covered with dust, but it seems all motionless things end up being covered in dust. I asked Jura if he thought it was time for me to vacuum the room. He scuttled into the corner. He's no use.

The nights became many-headed hydras, and our only choice was which maw to leap into, only to be chewed up and spit out in the morning. Maroje claimed that it had something to do with Hemingway's myth of the modern man. We can be destroyed but not defeated. It seemed to me that we simply did not know what to do with ourselves. Hemingway's man would have gotten up and continued from where he stopped. We just lay down and stared at the sky.

The air seems filled with spots. The air is sick. This doesn't bode well. Humankind might suffocate. Still, that's not so bad either. On the other hand, people are too wily to just give up on their right to live like that. They'd find a replacement for air. They've already managed to find a replacement for happiness.

And for reality. It's just a matter of time when air will become superfluous to them. To them. Them. You're one of them, you smug cunt, don't fantasize that you've gone rogue from this knocked-out world, that you are the one who isn't sliding down monochrome fields, obeying the rules.

My problem is that I can't lie. I can't even lie to myself. That's why I suffer so much because of girls, because I'm convinced every single one of them is my true love.

*

I try to be a good person, but, as a saint once said, the only consequence of that is a guilty conscience. So, I've decided to stop trying. At anything. I've decided to just be. And so, there I was, being, on my way home from the kiosk, with a cigarette in my mouth and the sun in my shades, and I saw a boy dribbling a basketball on the court in front of the building. He shoots, he misses, the ball bounces my way. I catch it. Jump shot. Nothing but net. A dagger. A three pointer. I blow off smoke, raise my arms, I'm the champion of the world. The boy gives me a dumb look, and I go on my merry way, as tall as the Empire State Building, high-fiving my shadow, never feeling the bones on which I was walking. MJ was right. Everything will be all right.

CHEWING GUM AND THE APOCALYPSE

Green eyes. My heart is beating like the rhythm to "Blue Monday." It's hard to read her emotions: sadness, maybe even longing; or plastic, pure disinterest. Even in the dark of the night club I can clearly see the color of her eyes. Everything around us is in fifth gear. Maroje tells me something, but my brain is currently not capable of deciphering the meaning of his words. Dead voices. Green, electric eyes. Her lips move.

What is it?

I feel like I know you.

Maybe from a past life.

It does seem like a past life.

A friend drags her away and they go to the ladies' room. The world drops back down to second or third gear, the music starts making sense, and Maroje's words are no longer dead air. Yes, I would like another beer.

For a moment, I thought someone had hypnotized you and that you were going to take all the money out of your wallet and give it to the mysterious hypnotist, Maroje tells me as we make our way to the bar.

I just thought I saw someone I knew. Turns out that I was staring at a complete stranger.

Maybe it was someone you knew in a past life, and the memory surfaced. Go to her, she might be the love of your life.

For a moment I considered it. I was once King Solomon, and the Song of Solomon is about her.

Or she was Solomon, the soul cares not about the body.

We finally make our way to the bar and order beer. Marin and Sven are talking to some girls and we head towards them, meeting a couple of acquaintances along the way. The night slowly melts away, and we head home on foot around two.

*

Black and white, stifling sweat, so many people, air, I need air, I'm dying. The floor is slick with sweat, urine, spilt beer, and vomit. I push my way through the crowd and instinctively find the door. I open it. The madness of the night dissipates in the soft morning light breaking through the green curtain of the treetops, in the silence of the breeze and the chirping of the morning birds. It's spring, I can recognize the scent. I'm on a playground where I used to play as a child. A girl is sitting on one of the swings. The prettiest girl I've ever seen. Wearing a white dress with black dots. Curly, brown hair, green eyes. Green eyes. They are looking at me. Green eyes. She's saying something to me, but the dream starts merging with the city morning, with the venomous asphalt reality. Her voice got lost in the jumble of drowsy thoughts. I curse the guy on the other side of reality.

"Who Loves the Sun" starts playing from my cellphone, my morning alarm, and I can't tell whether I was trying to be ironic or just plain stupid when I chose that song to wake me. Blurry. Black. Blurry. Black. Less blurry. I get up, turn off the alarm, put on my jeans and head to the bathroom. The radio is playing in the kitchen. Alisa was sitting at the table, reading a magazine and drinking coffee. I'd met Alisa the previous night, she studies at my college. We hit it off quickly. She lives in a dorm, and I told her she could stay at my place for a couple of days.

Good morning, I tell her and pour myself some coffee.

Do you even mean it? she says, without even looking up from the magazine.

What?

Do you want me to have a good morning?

When I say things like that, I'm not thinking about what they mean. I sit opposite her and take my first sip of coffee. The world becomes warm.

But?

But, obviously, I don't want you to have a bad day.

That's nice. Then I will wish a "good morning" to you, it actually means that I want your whole day to be nice.

I didn't say nice, just not . . .

Bad. And what does that mean?

You don't get splashed by a car waiting for a bus that's late, no pigeons crap on you, even though fools call it lucky, you don't get caught without a ticket on the tram, that sorta thing. Even if my day is nice, I don't expect to win the lottery, mostly because I never buy tickets.

So what *do* you expect?

I shrugged.

It would be nice to see a pair of green eyes.

But my eyes aren't green.

No, they're not, but that's okay, we don't know each other from a past life. I never wrote the Song of Solomon for you.

You know, sometimes you're hard to follow.

Tell me about it, I've been following myself my whole life and I still don't get me.

*

Blurry. Black. Blurry. Black. Less blurry. I see the ceiling. Okay, get up, stand up. It's somehow too silent, the radio isn't on, which means Alisa isn't home. Jeans, socks, straight to the bathroom. Grey marks on my face, time to shave. Hop, that was quick, just one cut. Just a flesh wound. In the kitchen, a note attached by a fridge magnet.

Elias,

I've gone to the store. Pale called, he wanted to remind you that he's playing tonight at the Factory and that you're on the list. Be back soon. There's milk in the fridge.

Alisa

I turn on the radio. Traffic reports from the streets of Zagreb. I make coffee. I know, it will be too bitter, I don't know how to make it like Alisa does. All the better, I'll wake up quicker. I can hear them shoveling snow outside my building. An idyllic winter image in the middle of the concrete housing of my neighborhood. Half-naked, I walk out onto the balcony; the air smells like firecrackers and cheap capitalist solidarity and generosity. I hate this time of year so much. I hate the snow, the Christmas sales, the smell of mulled wine and the drunks sitting in pools of their own piss in night trams. I also hate the neighbor who always offers me her freshly baked cookies. I feel bad because I can only give her a fake smile. The cookies *are* good, though, and she looks fantastic for a forty-year-old.

Alisa returns from the store. I help her with the bags. Snowflakes melt in her long brown hair. Her nose is red, her eyes brown and childlike.

I told you not to go to the store for me.

Oh, it's okay, you got pretty drunk yesterday, and, after all, it's the . . .

The holiday cheer, yes, yes. It drives me crazy, I can't wait for people to be back to their usual, selfish, asshole selves.

No hope for mankind?

Waits said: "If there's one thing you can say about mankind, there's nothing kind about man." So no, *nada, nichts.* Anyway, are you coming to the concert with me tonight?

She pours herself some coffee. She takes a sip.

Eww, pass the sugar.

I hand her the sugar bowl. So?

I can't. Going to the movies with a friend.

I go to my room and put on a Russian navy shirt. The Velvet Underground are playing on the radio; no, wait, it's Lou Reed on his own. "Perfect Day"—I can't understand how a cranky guy like Lou Reed was able to sing something like that. It makes me laugh. Alisa raises an eyebrow, but decides against asking me what I'm laughing about. I call Maroje and we make plans for the show. I tell him to remind Marin and Sven.

*

The boys from Heroina finish their show and the audience wants an encore. I stand at the side, over by the bar. A group of girls is in front of me, and one of them turns around. Green. Supernova. Thousands and thousands of stars disappear, someone sucks all the color out of the world, leaving behind only silhouettes. Thin, soft, black lines against a white, sterile backdrop. Between us, solitude and silence. Green eyes. Couldn't that color have vanished as well? Your clothes are white, your lips are white, but those eyes. They still look like spring.

Oh, hi.

I feel like I know you.

This feels like déjà vu.

From a past life?

Perhaps.

Your eyes are green.

Excuse me?

Look around you. Only silhouettes and whiteness. It's as if someone has erased all the colors.

You're hard to follow.

Tell me about it.

A flutter, a stroke of butterfly wings, a breeze that causes the hurricane which brings disaster. The colors and sounds start blending, a cacophony of colors, a palette of sounds. She turns around towards the stage, and I towards the bar. I try to phone God, to ask him to send an exterminator angel to kill me in all my past lives. Wrong number, you idiot, the Celestial Bureaucracy doesn't do reincarnation. And what now? Shiva, or whomever it is, doesn't believe in telecommunication. It's only a pair of green eyes. It's only a memory. The butterfly wings that might cause an apocalypse. A flood of thoughts. The children will scream, the men will console the weeping women, the priests will clutch their rosaries, and I'll be walking down the park, blowing bubble from a cheap chewing gum that loses its flavor after five minutes. Who cares? It's the apocalypse anyway. Five, four, three, fuck, the strawberry taste is gone. Silence, nothingness.

So, what now?

Another beer? Maroje asks.

Another beer, I nod.

THE PART ABOUT ALISA:
A TRIPTYCH THAT ISN'T

ALISA UNDER THE UMBRELLA

The diary said that the day could not have started better. A dark-haired, gangly young man lay on the couch. He traced out invisible lines with his finger pointed at the ceiling. Finally, we hear sound. The young man is humming, and a vinyl record is gently crackling from the speaker, playing Darklands by The Jesus and Mary Chain. On the table next to him, his I HEART NY mug is full of a black-brown liquid, and several LP covers are strewn on the floor around him.

I remembered the summer and the taste of salt on her skin. I remembered the evening when my guitarist and I lay on the roof, lit a joint, played some music from a cellphone and stared at the sky. We didn't count the stars, we talked about our failures, there were many more of those, it seemed. We talked about politics-music-movies, Zen, Hawking, and black holes.

Things started to change that summer. I frowned, trying to remember some milestones in my life. Things that may not have been dramatic, but helped shaped me. I sat up and listed my "top five milestones" in my diary. The list looked like this:
- Masturbating
- Punk rock
- *Monty Python*

- *The Lost Diaries of Adrian Mole*
- The Top Five lists from *High Fidelity*

After that I developed a habit of making Top Five lists of things. Top Five Music Albums, Top Five Songs for a Rainy Day, Top Five Driving Songs. I lay back on the couch and closed my eyes. When I opened them again, I glanced at my watch and started thinking about Top Five Excuses for Running Late. The list was uncannily similar to my big milestones in life:

- Masturbating
- Punk rock
- *Monty Python*
- Getting stuck in an elevator
- Running into a high-school acquaintance who just won't let you leave

*

In the dewy windows of the bus, the streetlights have halos; they look like tall, bony angels watching over the streets. Three halos blended and overlapped, reminding me of Mickey Mouse's head. I stepped out of the bus and headed towards the place I was supposed to meet Alisa. Alisa always had perfectly combed hair. Alisa didn't like snow falling on her perfect hair. Alisa had similar tics to mine; when she washed her hands, she would always soak and soap them up evenly. Alisa still had a childish, curious glow in her eyes, and wasn't aware of it.

Alisa and I always have these long conversations. After two or three words we'd know what the other person meant to say. She chain-smoked, forgot to reply to text messages, and tried to convince me to skip classes and go to the movies with her.

She answered some of my questions with a kind of shrug that made me laugh.

I saw her silhouette under a streetlight. She was holding up an umbrella to shield herself from the snow. I slipped under her umbrella. Hello, I say, hello, she answers. A couple of snowflakes have gotten tangled in her long, brown hair, and a couple more are spangled across her coat. I could make out the shapes of some of them, looking like tiny shurikens stuck in the wool or polyester. She was tapping one boot against the other. She couldn't let one boot get more snowy than the other. I knew well that sense of unease caused by asymmetry.

You're late.

Sorry.

*

There was nothing in the diary except for the date. The young man lay on the couch on his side. His eyes were shut, and there was an unrest under his eyelids that was a very clear sign that he wasn't sleeping.

I reach for the cup on the table and have a sip of coffee. It's cold and bitter. I get up and head to the bathroom to wash up and shave. I only cut myself once, that's okay, I've been known to do much worse. I reach for my toothbrush; its colors remind me of the tracksuits of Eastern European Olympic athletes in the eighties. I brush my teeth and stare in the mirror. Disheveled hair, bleariness clearing from the eyes, the circles under my eyes retreating: I look a bit healthier, but I'd still switch places with the person on the other side of the mirror. I wash up again, but there are still traces of felt tip pen on my left arm, the snow, the black snow that Alisa drew on my arm while we were both drunk at the party. I wipe my face with a towel and swing it across my back, head to my room, pick up the phone, sit on my bed, and dial her number.

Yes?

Her voice is nice over the phone. Hi, I reply.

Hi, Elias.

I don't know how I managed to get home last night.

Me neither. Luckily, I live ten minutes away from the university.

I walked behind some Gypsy woman.

I hear her lighting a cigarette.

I walked behind a Gypsy woman, and I could clearly see tracks in the snow, made by all the people who had walked that path before us.

She blows out smoke.

She was tracing other footsteps, leaving no trace of her own.

Mhm?

I don't know. I can't erase the snow you've drawn off my arm.

Are we going to the movies tonight?

What's playing in the art cinema, the one on Tuškanac?

I don't know, let's go in blind.

Okay. Half past seven in front of the cinema?

Sure. Bye.

I press the red button and put away my phone.

*

We stood in the university hallway for an eternity before I kissed her. Prior to that, the conversation had ended awkwardly, with her expecting a kiss and me babbling nervously, incoherently. Confusion comes naturally with her. She walked away to the students' club, and I had classes and had to go to the bathroom. The walls and doors were scrawled with messages, slogans, and song lyrics. I knew them almost by heart. I entered the bathroom, and the toilet bowl became my Madeleine cookie. Hazy memories of the Christmas party washed over my head, from the first to the final, fatal, beer. I shivered, flushed, and the water took away the memories along with the urine.

*

When I got out of class, the students' club was closed, the hallways empty. There were a couple of students outside, smoking and unsure where to go. My breath was steaming in the cold air. I usually search the steam for shapes and characters, as if it were a sort of vision, but now the characters are eerie serpentine silhouettes. I tighten my scarf and head towards the tram station. There are no stars in the sky, and the moon is in the gutter.

*

The bathroom is dark and out of soap. I've soaked my hands unevenly so I'm trying to rectify this. I stick out my left and then my right under the tap to even things out. The dryer is out of order, so I wipe my hands on my shirt. I walk out of the bathroom and pay for my espresso. The waiter absent-mindedly gives me my change and stares into the teletext: results from Belgian second league soccer. I put on my coat, walk out and head towards university. There's a poetry reading at the students' club. I find my place at the bar, order a beer and listen. Some guy is passionately reading his dismal poetry, trying to sound like a manic street preacher, but the only thing coming out of his mouth are empty phrases, dead voices without any inspiration. He finishes his first poem, rifles through his notes. And a weak applause comes from the audience. I turn back to the bar and focus on my beer. Boba is tending the bar.

So, Elias, what do you think?

It sucks.

Almost everything sucks to you.

I shrug.

The poet goes on, firing his bursts of blanks, and the night is deaf, disinterested. I finish my beer, pay for it, and walk out in the middle of a poem. The beginning of a new story starts forming in my head. Love is a selfish and jealous bitch who barks at everyone. Yeah, that's a good beginning, I say to myself as I walk out of the university building, too bad someone else has written it before me. I head home along a shortcut, talking to my shadow. I pass under streetlights which go out as I pass. The night is deaf, the streets are empty. Too bad, I say to myself, I'd love it if I could ask someone for the wrong way to get to Novi Zagreb.

YOU, ME, THE WHITENESS AND THE LATE NIGHT TRAMS

The long nights, lying next to each other wordlessly for hours.
And the snow, falling all night on the wounds of a generation
that can, once again, say only: Déjà vu.

J. Fauser

The sun had barely risen above the concrete blocks when I started making coffee. The morning light receded, the birdsong intertwined into a strange polyphony with the sounds of the passing cars. My shadow was stretching out beside me.

I'm having imaginary dialogues with Alisa, I told my shadow.

What do you mean?

I have prepared a lot of scenarios. I've planned it all out, the shots, the frames, the musical score.

Why?

So I'm not surprised. I know the theory, I just lack practice. I rehearse every day, talk to myself, I know all the scenes by heart.

You've lost the plot.

Maybe, but she won't surprise me.

But it's her role to bring confusion into your life.

I know, that's why I've prepared countless scenarios, I have a reply to every argument she can throw at me.

You think that will change things?

Excuse me?

You think she doesn't have a scenario mapped out as well?

See, I hadn't thought of that. I get the feeling that her scenarios are not the same as mine.

I get the feeling that she has only one scenario.

Thanks for the support, buddy.

Hey, I'm just being realistic, and anyway, you won't get caught off-guard.

And what now? I could prepare for every scenario she could throw at me, she was still going to catch me off-guard. With every second I was edging closer to that catastrophe, to the death of a relationship, to the fireworks and the absence of a happy ending. I go to the living room, throw myself on the couch and stop moving. I play dead, try to freeze time, all in vain: I can hear the damned clock ticking. I've got nothing to do but stick my head straight in the sand.

I'm cold.

Your windows are ajar.

You really think there's only one scenario?

Pal, I know everything there is to know about women.

Shadows have relationships?

Women have shadows too, don't they, you jerk?

I wasn't aware that other people have such hyperactive shadows.

Well, they're usually not so perky, but you can always find one if you try.

I took a sip of coffee and stared out the window: it was snowing, and the snowflakes were paper scraps with silly messages from you. Thousands and thousands of scraps with your thoughts on them. I stepped out onto the balcony, held out my hand and started catching the messages. They melted on my palm. I closed my eyes and stuck out my tongue; we used to do that together in front of the university building. The lady dusting her carpet from her balcony across the street looked at me as if I had lost my mind.

*

I lie in the snow and stare at the concrete sky, and the snowflakes cover my wounds. An old man with a shovel is struggling against the snow. He stops for a moment and looks at me.

Are you all right? He yells. Do you need help?

No, no, I'm fine over here, just peachy.

You'll get wet and catch pneumonia.

Many famous artists died of pneumonia. Chopin, for example.

Didn't he croak because of tuberculosis?

Tuberculosis, pneumonia, it doesn't matter, we all pass because of misery.

Who? artists?

Tsk, nah, I grumble, humanity in general.

Whatever you say, neighbor.

The snow keeps falling, I stay on the ground and absorb my thoughts. They take me back to a night when there was nothing except you, me, the whiteness and the late night trams.

PAPER PLANE DREAMS

If there was a unit to measure misery, it would bear my name
—Braca ("When I Grow Up, I'll Be a Kangaroo")

I think I've gone crazy, I say and scratch my cheek, irritated by my three-day stubble.

What are your symptoms?

Who are you, Freud?

Shut up. How do you feel?

North-by-South.

North-by-South?

North-by-South, between the North and the South.

He raises his eyebrows, his glasses slip a bit.

Torn apart, brother.

*

The sky was crazy, not me. It merged with the skyscrapers, it seemed as if I could touch it from the rooftops. It started snowing, and I fought my way through a blizzard. The night had taken a completely wrong turn, and my legs, leaden and heavy, kept tripping.

Congratulations, Elias, nicely done, my shadow tells me. Sometimes it's hard to say what you really feel.

Through the blizzard I could see the statue of Cardinal Stepinac in front of the high school I used to go to. I squint as the snowflakes slap my face and all I can see is the statue of the saint, covered in snow, the lanterns shining like fluorescent fireflies and the sky of a color which tells me there will be blood tonight. And I, an aging hitman, approach the statue, kneel in front of it, say a little prayer, get up, light a cigarette, and embark on what will probably be my last assignment in a life full of cigarette smoke, whiskey, and dangerous dames.

Not going to happen, I'm not a hitman, I'm not old, and I certainly don't intend to kneel in the snow. I pass by the statue, laughing and dancing, dancing down the street, and the tracks I leave confuse anyone following me.

*

We stood on a schoolyard, next to the benches by the basketball court. The clouds were speeding past faster than planes starships comets meteors. The snow was melting, a spring breeze was blowing. She was looking at me, waiting to hear what I would say, and I took off my coat, picked up a white dandelion and blew on it. Its seeds became paper planes with my thoughts written out on their wings. They got entangled in her hair.

Read them.

*

When I woke up, midnight had already come and gone. I made myself some instant coffee, sat at the table and stared out the window. Only my desk lamp was on in the room and, like a moth with its wings singed, I was completely disoriented, my dreams were running wild. Jura the spider was hauling his dust around. After a sip of coffee everything became clearer, and the characters from my dreams screamed as they disappeared.

*

The western sky is always at its prettiest the moment before the sun submerges below the concrete. I felt like I had been staring at it for too long. The phone rang, and I watched it for a couple of moments before picking up.

Hey, am I interrupting something? It's Sven, the guitar player in my garage band.

No, not at all, I tell him, and start doodling on a piece of paper.

I came across a couple of old blogs the other day.

Yeah?

Yeah, yours, mine, Tana's.

I went pale at the mention of her name. Tana is one of those girls you barely get over, and even when you do, at the very mention of her name, all the pictures, from the first time you met to the final "fuck off," come streaming through your head.

Yes?

Well, we've got a problem.

What kind of a problem? I ask him, as my scribbles turn into nervous creatures.

I have a feeling as if the past and the present were blending.

What do you mean?

I'm talking to you, but it's not you, it's an Elias from a couple of years ago.

Shadows?

Yes, shadows. As if nothing I can see or hear actually belongs here.

So? My creatures are ripping the skin off their faces like junkies in a fit of hysteria.

I don't know, it feels unpleasant, man.

Take a stroll, put on a coat, walk. Spring is just a couple of kisses away.

A couple of kisses?

Maybe it's a couple of songs, I'm not sure. Walk, observe, and write.

Okay, yes, maybe I should. Thank you.

You're welcome, bye.

Hey, wait, are we on for rehearsal on Friday?

Of course.

Ok, bye.

Hey, wait, don't forget to bring the effects pedal.

Okay, bye.

Bye.

*

We were standing under your white umbrella with red dots, nothing around us but snow. Just the snow and the wind that carried it. My hands were in my pockets, nervously scratching the skin off my fingers. I tried to catch the thoughts bouncing off the dark recesses of my consciousness, and your eyes, they choked the words in my throat. I dreamed about a neon kiss, feeling like I had already lived through all this. I finally spoke.

I've written a hundred pages of silence, I think you'll like them.

You were silent, growing ever more distant. The sky cracked into a thousand pieces and the snow caught on fire. I wake up in a cold sweat. After a minute of anxiety I get up, it's pitch black; I stumble, looking for my phone. The fingers find the keys on their own. I dial Sven's number, he should still be awake.

Hi, I say in a coarse voice.

Hi, you're still up.

Sort of. What are you doing?

Playing, reading, can't seem to rest.

Sven?

Yes?

That dreamcatcher.

What about it?

It doesn't work.

*

I turned off the TV. I wanted to throw it out the window. Just moments ago I'd heard the story of a young man, a thirty-something, homeless. He had lost his parents, had no friends, no girlfriend. He did have a college degree. But no job. He collects bottles. He said he dreamt of walking, clean and tidy, towards a classroom, a student register in his hand. I felt like crying, I don't want to become callous.

The Libertines sang that now was a time for heroes. Everything that's beautiful in the world—rock 'n' roll, poetry, prose—was hurtling to the bottom. Our heroes are mute and autistic, but they're among us, we just don't recognize them, and once we do, it will be too late.

Humanity is charging fanatically towards the abyss, and that's the best thing about all of this, when we burn up in an atomic cloud, there will be nothing left of us but the poisonous wind. We have enough atomic weapons to destroy the world twelve times over, and once is all it will take.

*

Alisa stood under her umbrella, smoking a cigarette. She was singing a song I'd heard a couple of days earlier on the radio. Her voice was pleasant. I approached her. She was wearing that red lipstick that made all the other colors look grey and boring.

Hello.

Hello.

I'm not late.

I can see, good on you.

It's not raining.

It's not.

It's not snowing.

You're right.

Why the umbrella, then?

I'm singing.

Oh, okay, if you're singing.

Where are we going?

I don't know, let's follow the green lights and walk on the shady side of the street.

ROADSIGNS

What's the furthest place from here?
It hasn't been my day
For a couple of years
what's a couple more?
                    —Blake Schwarzenbach

When I dial Alisa's number, a beautiful melody plays. I ride a tram to Novi Zagreb, leaning my head against the glass, and the speaker makes an unpleasant noise, crackling as if it's trying to tell me that there's no such thing as a next stop. We cross a bridge, and the sun shines on its metal railing. The sunlight reaches me in lazy waves; I squint, I frown, but I feel at ease. I like crossing bridges, it makes me feel as if I was leaving something behind.

*

I was arranging the books on my shelf, to create the impression that my life is less of a mess. I glanced at the floor. Various magazines, comic books, and several children's books were scattered around it; fifteen years of my life, scattered. I should have gotten rid of those, there was no more room on the shelves. I felt a bitter taste in my mouth, more bitter than when your girlfriend leaves you, more bitter than a hangover. I sat on the floor and picked up the magazine closest to me. It was a videogame magazine from 1999. As I leafed through it, images from my childhood flashed before my eyes: my best friend and I used to spend hours staring at the screen, until my mother or father said that that was enough, that it was sunny outside and that we should go out and climb some trees. There were also a couple of stolen issues of *Playboy* that we'd shared as kids.

That evening I made a pyre on the levee. I invited a couple of friends. We burned all our magazines and comics and watched the fire. It swallowed Tom Sawyer, Alice's rabbit along with some *Playboy* bunnies, Dylan Dog and Martin Mystère. They didn't scream, didn't panic; they knew they'd stay etched in our eyes. That night I discovered this: if you want to grow up, you have to preserve the child within.

*

Alisa never talks about her dreams. She used to tell me that she never dreamed, but that can't be true. We all run from something, and we run through our dreams. Everybody's got a reason to dream. I waited for the bus, studying the sun through the haze of my own breath, the snow was slowly melting, and a woman was standing next to me with a five- or six-year-old girl. The girl wouldn't stop talking and kept asking her mother questions.

Mom, I dreamed that I was a hummingbird.

How does such a tiny child know what a hummingbird is? I thought.

All right, dear, but dreams aren't real.

Since when? I thought.

The girl frowned and stared at the floor, drawing on the floor with the tip of her shoe. Her mother's phone rang; she told the girl not to move, walked a couple of steps away and answered the phone. The girl stood in place, shifting from one foot to the other as she kept drawing in the snow.

Hey, I said, and crouched next to her.

She gave me a suspicious look; My mom told me not to . . .

. . . Not to talk to strangers. But I'm not a stranger. My name is Elias.

She laughed. I'm Ana-Marija.

What are you drawing?

I'm not drawing, I'm doodling.

All right, what do you see in the snow?

She squinted. Africa, she said.

Africa?

Yeah, it's that country where black-skinned people live, and they wear colorful clothes and ride zebras.

Zebras?

Yes, it's a kind of black and white horse.

Are you sure they're black and white, and not white and black?

Yes, my grandpa told me so.

Your grandpa is a wise man.

Yes, he has a beard and everything.

I laughed. Ana-Marija?

What?

What your mother said, about dreams . . . that's not true: they are the other side of the looking-glass.

Like Alice?

That made me laugh.

Yes, like Alice, I said, and saw the bus approaching. Or like Alisa, I thought as I got on the bus.

*

Last night I stepped out into the rain and went to the other side of the city, north of the river. I couldn't sleep. On my bedroom wall I saw distorted faces, grimacing, screaming. I couldn't find Jura the spider to have a chat with him, so I got up, quickly got dressed and rushed out of the apartment. My umbrella barely shielded me from the downpour. The dead walked the streets, apparitions whose faces had been washed away by the rain, leaving only outlines. I closed my eyes. I heard the tram slide down the tracks, through closed eyelids I could see the neon lines it was leaving behind. I heard the electric crackling in the wires. I could hear the screams of my dreams melting and washing down the sewer drain. Thousands of screams melting while I hid under the awning of a kiosk and waited for my tram, the famous number 31 that's always going in the wrong direction. After two in the morning, all the trams only ever go in the wrong direction.

I've seen all of this before, I thought. Things don't change at all. Is every night, every moment déjà vu? I shuddered at the thought and laughed. The clerk in the kiosk gave me a confused look, but I paid him no mind; he doesn't know that above the closed, cruel sky, beyond the curtain of smog, the stars and the sun shine. Then the tram came, and it was almost empty. I sat down, leaning my head against the glass, and the speaker makes an unpleasant noise, crackling as if it's trying to tell me that there's no such thing as a next stop. A drunk sat across the aisle from me.

Son, is it still raining?

Yes, but the sun is still shining, we just need to unlock the sky.

He didn't hear me, but I think he understood me. Tomorrow would be a better day. Sometimes this world is more beautiful than we dare admit.

A BAD DAY FOR RED PANTS

and then let's hope that Heaven isn't
like those portents
of endless moments
of harp-playing
toothless poets
                    —P. Kvesić

It was the day when some generals were convicted. I had no clue about that. For me, the most important news in those days was a collaboration between the singer of The National and Cave's Grinderman. (The National and its army of fanatic followers had started to grate on my nerves; something must be seriously wrong with a band whose fans are such complete morons.) Great. So, that morning I was woken up by the ringing of my phone.

Yes?

Hey, you idiot, have you heard?

Of course I have. What a terrible song.

What song are you talking about? They took our generals away!

What do you mean, our?

Croatian.

I'm vaccinated against patriotism, sorry. In any case, I'm not Croatian. I don't feel the weight of my grandfather's bones or the burden of the soil in which they rot.

So what are you then?

An Inuit.

Fuck off. What was that about a song, then?

The singer of The National working with Grinderman.

You don't say.

Yeah.

Horrible.

Yeah.

Are we going out tonight?

After last night's havoc?

Yeah.

Okay.

Fine.

Bye.

*

Let's start with the sunset. It was running late. I explained that away by the days getting longer. Whatever it was, the sun's beams wrapped around the tracks, windows, store displays, glasses, everything. They twisted and dispersed. You could say that it was a perfectly ordinary sunset, of the kind common in spring and summer. It might have been more interesting had I watched it from a bridge or a rooftop, but from here it was ineffective at arousing my poetic side.

I sat outside, in a neighborhood café with a great view of the world rolling by. People were coming home from work, children from school, everybody rushing somewhere, looking for the place or the life where they belong. A poet would have detected the central conundrum of human existence in this scene. But alas, like I said, my poetic side was uninterested.

And there was also my third beer and Maroje who was already thinking about something stronger. We are rugged guys, real tigers, no lie. You don't want to mess with us, old boy.

Music makes you hungry.

I don't think I follow, Maroje says while trying to establish eye contact with the waitress.

This weekend Goribor is playing at the Swamp. Next week it's No Age at the KSET.

Yeah, so?

So if I intend to go see the gigs, I'll have to give up on my daily meals at university.

Because?

Because I'll be dead broke if I don't. Ergo, no ticket.

Two shots of wormwood schnapps, please.

No wonder I can't put on weight. I fast every other weekend in the name of rock 'n' roll. Will that make anyone think of me as a holy man, a mystic?

You're an idiot. The wormwood schnapps are here.

So are you.

Yeah, I am. Drink up.

We down the wormwood schnapps. It's hot, and it doesn't agree with us. I use the menu as a fan to cool myself off.

Where are we meeting Sven and Marin? Maroje orders two more shots.

The Main Square.

Didn't they have some sort of protest there just now?

How am I supposed to know that? Who cares anyway?

You're wearing red pants.

So?

So, I think right-wing people don't like boys in red pants. It's the color of communism, of the socialists, that sorta thing.

Red is also the color of the first stripe on our country's precious flag.

No matter.

You're right. Today is a bad day for red pants.

We drink up the wormwood schnapps. Maroje takes out a hundred Kuna bill. His parents sent him this month's allowance. This will be a good night.

*

On the Square, we try to avoid the horde of degenerate nationalists; no dice. Luckily, the only thing they managed to hurl at us were words. Words directed against our male pride (Faggots. Boooo.). We met Marin and Sven and headed for the Gjuro. A familiar atmosphere. An under-lit underworld with loud music. Something recent. Must have heard it on the radio. Marin goes to the bathroom to roll a joint. I scan the room. Two things catch my eye. Two girls. A brunette and a blonde. The blonde is facing the other way, but if she's half as fine as the brunette, it'll be fine.

Marin steps out of the bathroom. Let's step outside for a smoke. What was it that Sever once said? In these parts, the smoke is not from the hash, it comes from the blood. Maroje says he can't move at all. He and Marin decide to stay outside. Get themselves together. Even better, I think to myself. This way Sven and I can snag those two girls. Two versus two. A fair fight.

A familiar atmosphere. An under-lit underworld with loud music. Something recent. Must have heard it on the radio. We approached the girls. It started off pretty well. We didn't have the money to buy them drinks, but they didn't seem to mind. Good old-fashioned charm and a couple of literary quotes did the trick. It was a done deal.

But then something happened, something Marx would have called class struggle. I went to the bar to get a beer, Sven went to the bathroom, and when I turned back, I saw a bunch of short, stocky guys dancing around OUR girls. They were American. Unsightly but loaded with cash. Suddenly, the girls no longer knew us.

Fuck 'em. Sven sips on my beer. In the meantime, our friends outside have messaged us that they've gone home.

Cool down, Joe, I tease him.

Just look at them! Hicks, every single one. But as long as they got the cash . . .

Leave them be. The rage of the proletariat will catch up with them.

So, what now?

I shrug. Let's go home. There's nothing here for us to do. I head towards the exit. Sven grabs me by the shoulder.

Look there, he nods his head.

What?

Someone left an entire bottle of whiskey on the table.

So?

What do you mean, so?

You can't be thinking of swiping that.

Of course I am. Sven approaches the table and takes the bottle. Sorry, *bro*, you've been careless.

We'd taken a few sips before we noticed some sort of fuss among the bourgeois bastards who had stolen our girls. I soon put two and two together. It was their whiskey. I started pulling Sven by the sleeve.

What is it?

It's their whiskey. Don't look. Leave the bottle and let's go.

But it was too late. The gringos had figured out the plot. They started approaching us. We're fucked, I thought. Not only have they taken our girls, now they're going to go Rocky Balboa on our asses.

That's our bottle.

What bottle?

That bottle of whiskey.

What bottle of whiskey?

We're gonna call security.

You do that.

A bouncer approaches us. He doesn't quite understand what the gringo is saying.

What's going on here?

They want to take our whiskey, and we won't let them, and now they're threatening us, Sven says innocently.

Oh really?

Yes. I take over. My coworker is celebrating his birthday, and we wanted to buy some drinks for the girls. Those ones over there, I point at the brunette and blonde.

The gringos soon found themselves out on the street, and we were dancing with the girls again. Pretty wasted, and pretty cheerful. (Lesson: never fuck with the working class.)

What was that? The brunette asks.

Class struggle, baby. Anyway, what's your name? I never even asked you.

Marta.

Hi, Marta, I'm Elias.

This will be a good night.

*

Vanda called me and asked me to come over. She needs me, she said. Vanda had never said that before. To anyone. Vanda is usually the person other people need, a first-class altruist. I felt special when she said those words. I need you, please, come. I hastily got dressed and left the apartment. I found her alone in a darkened room. She was sitting on her bed, hugging a pillow, and eating Nutella straight out of the jar. With a spoon. A big one. The Smiths were playing. I took a look at the playlist on Spotify: nothing but the Smiths, Cowboy Junkies, Mazzy Star, and Jawbreaker.

So, you guys broke up?

She nodded as the spoon bobbed between her lips. I sat next to her and hugged her. I didn't know what else to do. Empathy was never my strong point, since I was an egocentric adolescent who thought that bad things only happened to him. Everything happens to me, that's what Chet and I sing. Chet Baker, that junkie whose voice sounded just like his trumpet. And so I hugged her and talked nonsense. It wasn't very soothing. I somehow ended up in the middle of a kiss, and she was pulling me on top of her. Soon the problem wasn't that she was pulling me on top of her, but that she was pulling me into her.

I don't have a condom.

It doesn't matter.

What do you mean, it doesn't matter?

I want this.

Well I don't. I'm too young to become a demographic.

I soon found myself out on the street. My mission to console Vanda had taken a wrong turn somewhere. The city was covered in darkness. Many streetlights on her street didn't work. At the tram station I bummed a cigarette from a guy who was my age. Yes, I'd stopped smoking, but the image of tiny Eliases and Vandas disturbed me greatly. Oh well, I thought, the kids would be pretty and so damn smart. I often find people to be inscrutable and disturbing. It all boils down to sex. Reproduction. Pure demographics. Duty to your country. I just want to cuddle and use a condom during sex. It's somehow more romantic to me.

*

I missed the revolution. I don't know why I just remembered that.

That was last summer. When I woke up, the fences were torn down, and the barricades conquered. There was no heroism left for me, and I didn't mind. The last couple of years have been marked by people on the streets and torn vocal cords. For the first time, the slogans did not sound hollow to me. This particular incident was caused by some fat cat with too much money lying around whose dick got hard at the thought of an underground parking lot in the old center of the city. It was a classic case of David versus Goliath and, if what we tell our children were actually true, this story would not have ended the way it did. But I'm getting ahead of myself; like I said, I overslept our charge at the Bastille.

Between the torn-down fences, camps sprouted: some called the protesters lazy bums, while I saw the best minds of my generation stripped of their illusions about democracy. I saw the best minds of my generation not buying the spiel that other people know best what's good for us. They were called lethargic revolutionaries and posers. The insults and the insensitivity caught me off guard once again.

I remember us taking shifts to prevent the forces of mutated capitalism from eroding this town like a virus. We failed. One morning, in the early hours, just like in the worst dictatorial regimes, they came, picked up the protesters and hauled them off to jail. I, of course, overslept everything once again. When I got there, the construction work had already started. The police weren't hauling away anyone in riot vans. There was no more room.

I stood, disbelieving, watching the drills and excavators tear through the city asphalt. There was nothing I could do. And it had seemed like we would change the world and bring on a Copernican revolution in our consciousness. I'll never learn.

*

It was the day when the Pope came to Croatia. Absolute bedlam, I tell you. These here are against it, those over there are for it. I could say that I was indifferent. But I wasn't. I couldn't understand why they were making all this fuss about a wrinkly old man parading around in a sheet carrying Saint Nick's staff. Closed streets, restricted movement, cops everywhere, and all that for fear that someone might try to off the old man.

In any case, I tried not to get annoyed more than necessary. I missed out on a Catholic upbringing: I never found a common tongue with teachers in my religion classes. I believed in a sort of cosmic push-me-pull-you, what-goes-around-comes-around gravity that rules the world. That was the only thing that made sense to me, everything else seemed like a sugar pill for frightened folks attracted to the idea of eternal life. It doesn't really do anything for me. Listening to angelic *Glorias* and *Hallelujahs* all the way to Kingdom Come.

So, the whole nation was spiritually awoken, and I was getting tipsy by the bar at the Thalia. Crazy, crazy, Marin would say. He himself was tipsy by the bar, even though he was raised in a conservative Catholic family. He didn't care about tradition. A real progressive man. So cosmopolitan.

I was eyeing a girl. Like all the girls at the Thalia, she tried hard to look disinterested. Nothing to it, it's important not to let yourself get discouraged. I approached her. I said who I was. I threw around a couple of literary quotes, told her that I was a writer and that I played in a band. She was interested.

So, we had been talking for a while when I asked her if she wanted to step outside to get some air.

I have a boyfriend.

So? I'm not the jealous type.

He'll be here soon, and he doesn't like other guys hanging around me.

I shrugged. There's no greater waste of time than using up all your charm in vain on a random girl in the night. The next morning she vanishes in a hungover haze, and you feel relief that all of it didn't end up being just temporary pleasure. Still, the right girl is here, just around the corner. At least she could be.

I stepped out to get some air, a late revolutionary and failed Casanova. I realized that I would need to change something, either the world or myself. They say it's best to start with the little things.

THE GODS MUST BE
KNOCKED OUT

Not much had changed over the last couple of months. I still didn't know what to do with myself. I didn't know if I was still in love with Alisa. Dinamo kept losing, the newspaper headlines were still both a) depressing and b) sensationalist, and neither my street, my town, nor this world had any heroes. Still, it would be dumb to say that everything was the same. My band had broken up. Sven said that he couldn't play anymore. I reacted very maturely to his decision. I told him to go fuck himself, called him a traitor and told him not to call me anymore. Winter's frozen fingers moved on southward. The days were getting noticeably longer, and as the days grew longer so did my manuscript. I let Maroje read it.

Sometimes it's too infantile, childish, he says as he takes a cigarette out of his pack, stepping out of the university building.

I'm twenty, I can't sound too serious.

True, but you only write about girls, music, and nights out.

Is there anything more beautiful in our lives? I repeat, I'm twenty, I'm not capable of writing about something I don't understand. I don't want to be one of those frustrated kids who write as if they're eighty years old. I don't want to be a dead writer.

Except for that, you write pretty well. Your energy can be felt.

We sat on the steps in front of the university, and as the sun's rays slapped us around, we watched squinting as spring sneaked timidly down the street. Tibor was supposed to be there soon with the weed. We decided to light up before the last lecture. He messages us to meet him behind the university building, at our usual spot. Soon, he arrives, joint already rolled, perfect. I lean against the wall, inhale, blow the smoke out, pass the joint.

What shape are you trying to give to the smoke? Tibor asks me in between puffs.

The faces of girls, Maroje says as he passes me the joint.

That's not true, I say as I inhale, exhale. I try to avoid them.

That's why you write about them. All the time, Maroje keeps teasing me.

What is he supposed to write about as a twenty-year-old? Tibor comes to my defense.

Every girl is a great love story to him.

That's true, I join the conversation. I fall in love every day. It's not important whether I fall in love for five minutes or five months. It's not important whether I've fallen in love with a girl I just saw for the first time or a girl I've known for years, it's important that I'm smitten.

We go to class. Tibor is completely out; that's what regular smoking does to you. His eyes are like a battered boxer's. Maroje tries to focus on the lecture. I've decided to doze off. I snap out of sleep a couple of times; Tibor laughs at me. I go to the bathroom, slap myself with some cold water. I stare at myself in the mirror, I stare at my large eyes, currently a couple of sizes larger. I look scared. Several people have told me that I'm constantly running, through my poems, through my prose, through the many trenches I've dug for myself over the years. I'm not running away, I'm just dodging the blows, dancing around my opponent just like Muhammad Ali. He didn't become the greatest by charging the opponent like a bull at a red piece of cloth. He became the greatest by using what no one but Jack Johnson had used in the ring: his brain. Suddenly I became painfully aware of time: I had stared into the mirror for an eternity. I stepped out into the hallway, stretch, and try to get my thoughts in order. Line up!

I saw Alisa, tall and raven-haired, walking confidently down the hall. She was heading toward me, and I panicked. She must have seen me stepping out of the bathroom, so I couldn't dart back in. The only thing I could do was turn around and escape down the stairs, which isn't cool at all. So, hands in my pockets, I boldly go forward. She's smiling at me. For Christ's sake, why is she doing that? She has practically been avoiding me for the last month, or maybe even two.

Hello, she waves to me.

Hello, I wave to her.

I got a scholarship in Moscow!

On the 8th of March, 1971, New York's Madison Square Garden provided the stage to a fight (called the Fight of the Century) between Ali and Frazier. Ali kept provoking Frazier: "You can't beat me, don't you know I'm God." A second before he punched Ali with the force of a hundred megatons, Frazier told him "Lord, you're in the wrong place tonight."

I don't remember what I told her. I must have mumbled something about being happy for her, wished her luck and asked her when she was leaving. I don't remember what she said. The gods were knocked out, and I was left standing in the hallway, for a long, long time. The best thing about it is that it's painless, that's how I knew it was beginning, I remembered what Hemingway said. The pain came a couple of months later, with a postcard from the Red Square.

*

I walked out of the Wrong Way bar drunk, and headed to the tram station. It was the same station where I kissed Alisa for the first time . . . or did she kiss me? Where our words were left frozen, covered in snow. I leaned against the streetlight and waited for the night tram. My thoughts snaked erratically through my brain, and I remembered Judy Garland singing "Somewhere over the Rainbow" and tears started welling up in my eyes. Liquor makes you too sensitive. Some people become painfully honest or painfully dumb, shedding their armor and running naked in front of everyone. A horrible sort of exhibitionism. Others become dark creatures, angry and thirsty for blood. Not me; I simply become a fool.

I raised my chin and closed my eyes, and the newfound darkness spun like a ballerina. I opened my eyes and saw the snow falling. Huge, colorful snowflakes. One landed on my palm, inscribed with the words: "You're late." I suddenly realized that the snowflakes were frozen words, mine and Alisa's. I let the snowflakes melt. I sat down on the asphalt and let the words slowly cover me.

I get anxiety attacks in a hallway of mirrors, unsure if I'm on the ceiling or on the floor, left or right. I'm not sure on which side of the mirror I'm standing—am I just a sum of other people's fears? The glass cracks, the shards scatter like shrapnel, and I realize I'm falling towards the asphalt, which isn't going to embrace me; it will crush me.

The tram passes right in front of my nose, and I realize it's morning, around dawn, although the sky is more night than day, the moon still shone, and not a soul was out on the street. The nightmare is still shaking me, but the hangover curiously decided to spare me. I start the day with a net difference of zero, which is more than most people can say.

ROBBIE'S NOT IN LOVE, JOEY IS JUST FINE, AND I'VE BEEN FAKING IT FOR TWENTY YEARS

Robert Smith was singing about not being in love, Maroje was leafing through an issue of *Uncut*, and I couldn't understand why they'd placed anemic MTV bands in the same category with Pavement, Modest Mouse, and Mogwai. I found a new reason to hate the world just a bit more. Those days I tried not to look for nice things, precious moments, the small victories which I usually used to break through the morning and slide into a new day feet first. I was doing pretty well.

My horoscope, though, wasn't going gentle on me. In fact, that celestial bestiary was doing its best to sodomize me. I wasn't ready to give myself over to a higher power, I was a completely atypical Virgo, messy and nowhere near meticulous, and it was quite possible that that was the source of those cosmic gut-punches, from my band—which I had considered to be just the thing that rock 'n' roll was missing—breaking up, to Alisa moving to Moscow. I had thought that the story of me and Alisa was just the thing that literature was missing. My ambitions stayed the same, year in and year out. Every year, in every way, I was drifting further and further away from accomplishing my goals. I realized I'm not the thing rock 'n' roll is missing, I'm not going to save my generation.

Are you having fun? A woman's voice in front of me.

What?

I said, are you having fun talking to yourself?

It was a short girl, with short, tussled black hair. Around her big black eyes, I could clearly see traces of smeared make-up, and a somewhat lighter shade of bags under her eyes.

No, I'm not. I mostly manage to rile myself up.

That's no good.

None at all.

Do you take yourself seriously?

That's just about the only thing I don't take seriously.

How do you manage to rile yourself up then?

I'm not sure that's a conversation I want to be having with a stranger.

I'm not a stranger, my name is Megi, holding out her hand.

Hello, Megi. I'm Elias. We shake hands.

Why were you frowning?

They placed the Kings of Leon on the list next to Modest Mouse. It's like looking at a screaming neon supermarket next to a family store owned by a nice married couple.

Are you trying to say that the former don't have a soul?

Something like that, yes. Also, the former are slowly sucking the life out of the latter.

That's not very nice. It's kind of vampiric.

It's not nice at all, but I'll tell you something a wise man told me once: "So it goes."

What's the difference between these two bands?

Except for their earnings?

Yes.

I considered the question. I could kiss to the background of a Modest Mouse song.

And the Kings of Leon wouldn't work?

I was in a club once, the Kings of Leon started playing, and I started laughing, mid-kiss. The girl thought I was laughing at her and she wouldn't even look at me anymore.

So which other bands could you kiss to?

A fantasy of mine is to kiss to Jawbreaker's "Accident Prone" in a dimly lit room. Another is to kiss someone I'm not supposed to, to the sounds of "Ever Fallen in Love" by the Buzzcocks.

You sound like a young man with clear and realistic life goals.

Actually, nothing is clear to me, most of the time I don't know what I'm doing. I'm a natural born jazzman, I improvise all the time.

Maybe you've got some form of Tourette's syndrome, one that affects your entire life.

I've never thought of it that way.

Do you have a band?

I used to.

What happened?

We broke up, on the verge of releasing a vinyl.

Creative differences?

Laziness.

Oh. What did you sound like?

At first, we were dark and frustrated. But that wasn't me. That wasn't us, so we decided to get back to the roots.

The Beatles?

No, the Ramones. Rock 'n' roll begins with the Ramones.

Some would say that it begins with Iggy Pop.

Ooof, you're right.

One-nil for me?

A volley, right into the back of the net.

Recommend me a CD.

I looked at the shelves with the CDs. Then I looked at the LPs.

Why not a vinyl?

My brother's got that covered, I need you to recommend me a CD.

I thought about it and grabbed *Good News for People Who Love Bad News* by Modest Mouse.

Why them?

I often hear people calling a singer or a mediocre songwriter a "poet." It's usually guys who sell their overly sentimental verbal diarrhea to teenage girls. Not this guy, though. You can feel the energy, you can feel that there's more to his lyrics than the rhythm, the melody and some corny story.

Sounds interesting. Want to listen to it together?

I realized that she was inviting me over to her place. I explained to her that I was in a relationship, which was a lie, and that I was there with a friend, which was true. She smiled at me and told me to get in touch. I asked her where I could find her, and she told me that it all it would take is making the first move, setting out to find her, and after that, things would sort themselves out. She stood on her toes and gave me a kiss: she decided to buy the CD. I waved at her as she was leaving the store.

What was that about? My Shadow stared at me, arms crossed.

I never miss a chance to miss a chance.

Elias?

Yes?

Say "one-two."

One-two!

Fuck you!

And suddenly I realized where I was at. The time of myths

was long gone, my generation was late, we missed out on rock 'n' roll, the New Wave, brotherhood and unity and a bunch of other meaningless words that lost people cling to like a liferaft. Suddenly everything was clear to me, we've got nothing to mourn, everything behind us amounted to a great big nothing, and we were stuck in this moment, like insects in amber, trapped, eyes aimed at the sky, as if the hand of some higher power was about to draw a plan for our futures up there, give us all the right answers; eyes aimed at the sky, instead of looking at the horizon, where the sky meets the asphalt, instead of creating something that would be ours and ours alone, something that wouldn't let itself become bound by cheap phrases and dead words.

Joey Ramone sang about a wonderful world, Maroje was done leafing through his copy of *Uncut*, and I realized that opportunities presented themselves every day; I was just too dumb to recognize them. And I say to myself, what a wonderful world.

ROKY RAMONE

I've seen my share of talents and I met my share of clowns
—Natural Child

The vertical line on my screen flickers, messaging me in Morse code that I've got nothing to say. Nothing strikes terror into my heart as much as an empty sheet of paper, even if it's in pixel form. The absence of rhythm, strained vocal cords, gurgling sounds coming from my mouth. I light a cigarette, tap my fingers on the desk; a breeze is dancing a slow dance with the blinds, and I notice I already had a lit cigarette. I massage my eyelids with my thumbs, and when I open my eyes, the first sentence will materialize thanks to a misplaced act of divine providence, and there will be no more problems.

Nothing.

I exhale smoke and pace across the room. My cellphone rings. It's Pale, who tells me there's a party tonight in the apartment/studio of his photographer friend. Fine, I say, who's going to be there? He starts listing the names; I recognized a few and could only tolerate one. A designer and comic book artist, on the editorial board of a magazine I quite like. Not pretentious at all. He never makes unsolicited speeches about his work. About how difficult it is to create, or about how he does it.

I play a song by the Spits. They remind me of the Ramones

and I lie on the floor. I blow off some smoke and flick the ash on the floor. When I'm single, my responsibilities and hygiene go out the window. I walk around naked. I shower only before going out. I leave the toilet seat up. I eat straight from pots and pans, which pile up in the sink. I survive exclusively on pasta and omelets. I close my eyes. Scattered caravans pass under my eyelids. Neon tits on a horny nun; domes of mythic buildings covered in snow; hopscotch courts that stretch over entire neighborhoods like labyrinths that vanish after the first rain; a dog singing "Needles & Pins" by the Ramones. I open my eyes. It's getting dark. I take a look at my watch. I might as well go to the party. I won't be writing, that's for sure. A cold shower washes the hopscotch courts away, melts the snow, makes the nun even wetter, but the dog is still there. It is grinning like an idiot and wagging its tail.

Who's that? I ask my shadow.

Roky.

Like Rocky Balboa?

No, like Roky Erickson.

His dog has got two heads.

But it can't sing the Ramones.

I find myself in the city. I can't recall the bus ride, my body navigates on autopilot, warning me in advance of objects in my way and which present an immediate danger. A breeze blows from time to time, swinging the sky, blue on one side, dusty and kind of beat up on the other, and touching the skyscrapers, cranes and everything, the whole world is a bit askew.

I buy a bottle of red wine at a store. The wine is cheap enough so I can afford another box of cigarettes, since the night is long and often falls in with the morning, yet expensive enough that I can drink it straight, without cola. I decide to walk to the apartment even though it's fifteen minutes away.

On my way there, I give some change to kid playing guitar on the street. That's for not playing "Wonderwall." Further down the street, a blonde girl stops me. Says she's trying to save money to publish a book of poetry. I ask her what her poems are like, and she says they're optimistic.

No way, I tell her, I can't stand optimistic poetry.

After that I feel bad. I barge into the first bar I find and ask the bartender to open my bottle for me. I order a wormwood schnapps, slam it down, and pay with the change I had left. I walk out, lean against the wall and take a gulp. Why the hell did I need to be so rude to that girl? I walk up to her and tell her that I'm out of money, but that we can share a few sips of my wine. She accepts. And so we drink, leaning against the wall, smoking, blowing smoke into the darkening sky, while the breeze still swings it around.

What do you do? she asks me.

I write.

What?

Newspaper articles, and prose.

Really? You're a writer?

Sort of. I've only got a couple of short stories published.

I hope you get all of it published.

I hope you do, too.

I wish her luck again and head toward the apartment. My designer friend Momo meets me at the door. KEEPIN' BUSY, ZIZI? He's the only one who calls me Zizi, devil knows why. He's already kind of tipsy. He hugs me and shows me around the apartment. I see a couple of familiar, extremely unlikable faces. Writers. One of them asked me once how I wrote. Mostly, I sit down and type, I told him, usually while dressed. He looked at me with a mix of pity and wonder, as if I were a village idiot, and started talking about how, before every act of creation (those were his words), he played some Miles Davis or Coltrane and dimmed all the lights in his room. That's great, I told him, I'll go get some more beer. I notice there are a lot of pretty girls here. And everyone is so well dressed, their clothes talking for them: I like Godard, I've read everything Kundera has ever written, I think Baldessari is God, Barthes was a genius even though he couldn't move a step away from his mother. I'm not bitter, but I like to think I am. My clothes say that I don't give a fuck about anything. My underpants, however, say something else: I'm eaten away by thousands of tiny, bizarre insecurities. What's important, then, is that nobody sees me in my underwear.

I run into Pale and we hug warmly. We haven't seen each other in a couple of months. He's been busy with the band, I've been busy writing, or at least looking for excuses why I wasn't writing as much as I should. We sit on a windowsill, which has a view of the railroad tracks and the people in the streets who look like silhouettes against a negative image. The photographer's dog wanders around the apartment, and keeps approaching me and Pale. As soon as it comes near us, we turn into children, petting it and babbling incoherently. The dog uncomfortably reminds me of Roky: it constantly stares at me with its glassy eyes which glimmer with an almost angelic love.

We talk. He says he would love it if I went on tour with them, to cover it as a journalist. I'm getting more and more drunk, and my tongue starts getting twisted around my teeth. Pale's girlfriend comes around. I soon become uncomfortable, so I walk away. Passing me by, Momo hands me a spliff, and I take a hit. My feet are no longer on talking terms with the floor, my brain is stuck to the ceiling, my fingers are on fire. I take another hit, gulp down the last sip of my wine and decide that it would be for the best if I took a nap. I find a room with a mattress on the floor, surrounded by empty cups which, judging by the foam, used to contain beer. The remnants of the foam look like horrified faces, petrified victims of the Medusa. I lie down, close my eyes, and feel the darkness in my skull expanding like space, a huge blotch of ink. I open my eyes and see the dog sitting next to me with his tongue out.

What do you want? I ask him.

To tell your fortune from the beer foam.

Go on, then.

You are fascinated with untranslatable words.

What does that have to do with my fortune?

Komorebi.

Oh, I get it.

Really?

No, not really.

It means the interplay between the sunlight, the branches and the leaves.

A broken sky. Okay, I get it. What of it?

You will stare at that sky and gradually realize that it is getting more and more distant.

What else?

Iktsuarpok.

Uh-huh.

Do you know what it means?

What do you think?

It is a feeling of anticipation that makes you look at the door or through the window to see if anyone is coming.

Okay, what of it?

That will haunt you as well.

And? Will anything show up?

Sometimes. It's about the perseverance.

What about love, happiness, and all the rest of the astro-bullshit?

Do you really think I can read that in beer foam?

What do I know?

You can go ahead and carve longer lines in your palms if you think that will result in more favorable astro-geometry.

Do I look like Corto Maltese to you?

You'd like that, wouldn't you?

Sometimes. Is that it?

Good night.

Thank you.

I don't know why I thanked him. The dog was gone. I closed my eyes. The universe was still expanding.

VOLVOX DON'T GLOW
IN THE DARK

She claimed that I never listened to her or something like that. It wasn't anything serious, she wasn't mad, she just arrived at the conclusion that I had trouble concentrating. The sun was being born, the water for coffee was boiling, the waves were murmuring and caressing the sand. The sound made me want to pee. The sun was being born and she claimed I never listened to her. I went to pee.

I heard the spoon clinking against the cup.

Have you decided?

What?

Are you going home or not?

Should I stay or should I go?

She says something to me again, but I can't hear her over the stream. I yell.

What?

I said: I knew you'd find me.

I can feel her warm breath in my ear. We're in a nightclub, some sort of EDM is rumbling in the background and I can barely hear her. I answer by taking a sip of beer. Since we ran into each other at the record store, I haven't been able to get her out of my mind. The miniature hurricane who told me to call her Megi.

Who are you here with?

My brother.

The one who collects LPs?

What? She can't hear me.

The one who collects LPs? I yell in her ear. Her perfume is not intrusive. I like that.

Shall we step out?

Sure, I say. I'm going to take a piss, wait for me outside. She nods. I go to the bathroom. The men's room is not crowded. I'm done quickly. I zip up and go out.

She's drinking coffee. She hands me my cup. The sun is growing up fast. It's no longer a bloody newborn.

I told you, you don't have to go.

I answer by taking a sip of coffee. I ask her if she wants to go to the beach with me. She says she doesn't. She will drink coffee on the veranda and do crossword puzzles, or Sudoku. I take my towel and my book of Hemingway's short stories, and sit at the table.

You like to be at the beach when there's no one there.

I don't like the noise, the kids screaming.

I like the sound of children playing.

I shrug and take a sip of coffee. I kiss her on the cheek. I won't be long, I say. I walk out and head to the beach, about thirty meters from her house. I spread out my towel and lay Hemingway on it. I wade into the sea. It is cold and I shudder; my body instinctively wants to go out. I dive in and decide to swim to the buoys. I flip over to my back and let the waves rock me. No point in tensing up, just close your eyes. Relax.

I wasn't sure how long the kiss lasted. Maybe just a second, maybe several hours had passed and dawn had already broken.

I like you, you're a good kisser.

I prefer Marica from second grade. Her socks didn't slip to her ankles like yours do.

Does she kiss like I do?

I hadn't heard that verb, "to kiss," in a long time. Everybody uses other, disgusting expressions.

Such as?

"Hooking up." It sounds so mechanical.

So, does Marica kiss as well as I do?

Who's Marica?

She laughs, twirls on her heel and heads towards the club. I follow her and get in. Megi is still doing the crosswords. I leave my book at the table.

I'm going to hit the shower.

There's no hot water, she yells.

Doesn't matter. I stand under the shower and let the water run: it is lukewarm, like summer rain. That sounds so soppy. Like summer rain! Doesn't matter, the feeling is good. Salt mixed with the water from the shower glides down my body in snaking curls.

We're caught in the rain, so we run to the nearest doorway. I push her against the wall. I can taste the dirty rain on her lips. I tell her that. She pushes me back, against the opposite wall. She says it's good that her brother can't see us. He can't stand anyone touching his sister.

I'm an outlaw, I do what I want.

Prove it.

I think about it, looking over the surnames on the intercom. I slide my fingers across all the buttons. I wink at her and run to the next doorway. Repeat. We run down the street. The lights go on in the apartments, people start looking out their windows. The streets are empty. They can only hear our laughter.

We walk around the Mediterranean town. We even dare to hold hands. It's a bit strange as she's so much shorter than I am. We mostly keep quiet. It's a pleasant silence. It's a form of communication, really. Everything is okay, you don't have to tell me, I know. We walk and soon we come back to her house, I tell her I'll go to the beach for a while. She will wait for me.

I promised to drop by at her place, so now I'm climbing up to the Old Upper Town. The city lies spread beneath me, the windows twinkle like plankton, like volvox or whatever, on the surface of the sea. The moon is so close I can grab its horn. I reach out my hand and close my eyes.

Do you plan on spending the night here? Megi sits next to me, her arms around her legs, shivering.

No. The sand isn't as warm as you.

Come on inside, then.

I'll stay a couple more days, I tell her; I get up and kiss her. The sea spreads out behind me, almost black. On its surface, the shimmering plankton, volvoxes or whatever. The moon is so close I can grab its horn.

THE MOON, A DRUNKEN HOMER AND THE ZERO-G TANGO

How many words, how many nomenclatures for one and the same confusion.

—J. Cortázar

You're not consistent. You don't know what you want.

I'm consistent when it comes to inconsistency and no, I don't know what I want, I know something much more important.

What?

I know what I don't want.

Sometimes I get the feeling that every day I'm talking to a different person.

That's because with every blink of the eye I become someone else.

I think you're finding excuses for yourself.

And I think you're too uptight. Relax.

What about Megi?

What about her?

Eighteen missed calls.

Megi has turned into eighteen missed calls? Interesting.

If you keep sabotaging yourself, she will turn into a single missed call.

Relax, man.

When my inner monologues—or dialogues with my shadow—started annoying me, I knew I couldn't go on like that. Outside, the summer was dying. The sunlight no longer pierced to the bone, it merely tickled the skin. I listened to music and pretended the songs were about me. It was the height of sentimentality, soppiness for art's sake.

Everything led back to the Doppler effect again, the glow was fading. Everybody is a world of their own, and sometimes these planets pass each other by, or even collide. The gravitational fields shift, the sky changes colors as if it were tripping, but we all know that planets never stay still, so relationships change. Two planets move away from each other, get closer to others, depending on their speed. It's pure physics. It's the alphabet of interpersonal relations. The art of forgetting.

I looked at the window. The blinds were down, the light was nimbly sneaking into the room, shooting its thin rays across it. I saw every dust mote. I walked up to the window and rolled up the blinds. The sun was tired, I could see traces of an almost reddish light on the building across the street. I squinted. These were the last warm days of the year; the sun would get smaller and smaller in our sky. Winter will be here soon. I considered switching the north for the south, like the birds do. I decided to follow the swallows. The birds are excellent navigators; Noah and Leif Erikson were no fools when they placed their hopes on the doves and ravens.

But even with smart navigators, there's a thousand ways to fuck things up: the correct answers are always few and far between. It's incredible how we endure, all those defeats and shipwrecks. The scratches become gaping wounds, and we persevere, growing number and number to the pain, our own and that of others. We become numb. It all boils down to whether you'll make it out of bed. After you do, everything is okay.

The phone rang. I listened to that shrill melody for a long while. The wrong answer is not the worst thing that can happen to you. Sometimes it's enough not to do anything.

Are you gonna pick that up?

It's not for me.

It's for you.

I'm going through a crisis of identity. I'm a magic marker. Magic markers can't answer phone calls.

Those days I was everyone and everything. I was the absence of light in a room with books scattered on the floor. I was Homer, too lazy and too drunk to sing the praises of mighty heroes and cities. I was the first student on the moon, swaying in a zero-G tango. I was that annoying inch between your hand and whatever you're reaching for, making you stand up to grab it. And Megi? Megi didn't call me the next day. Megi became a missed call.

ZAGREB, JE T'AIME

THE DREAM AND THE MELTING GLACIERS

I'm in love with a girl who doesn't exist. I don't know what she looks like, but last night in a dream I heard her voice. She called me and we talked. Her voice melted all the glaciers floating within me. She caused global warming, floods, all that jazz. I wake up in the darkness. Her voice is still ringing out in my head. It's so warm. I don't know who she is, but I have to find her. I stand next to the window and smoke, overcome by loneliness. I light my cigarette on the gas stove. I left my lighter at the bar last night. The night is quiet. The night is soft. Just me and the sounds of the cigarette burning down. I go back to bed. I look for her in every dream. I don't find her.

I tied the laces on my sneaker; it kept untangling. They were red Converses which I hadn't worn since the last day of high school. The wind was blowing and it looked like it would rain. Dust got in my eye. No trams in sight. But I was in no rush. I knew the voice on the other side would wait for me. It was just a dream, you'll say. Maybe. Maybe the boy on the other side was leading a better life. Maybe I was just one of his dreams.

How do you find a person who might not exist? I didn't know the answer to that, but I've always liked impossible missions. There's always something romantic about charging at windmills.

THE BOOK OF DREAMS

He called me and told me he would be late. It had turned into a habit of his. It wasn't a commendable trait, but it didn't bother me. I told him I would be waiting for him at the bookstore. So there I was, leafing through the books that had titles that I liked. But the letters kept rearranging, spelling out last night's dream. I had tried to forget it, but somehow everything was doing its best to remind me of it. After several years without any dreams, yesterday I dreamt. It didn't mean a lot to me. But I guess it did to others, since they were doing their worst to make me remember the dream.

Oh well, since the letters themselves are rearranging, why not?

My diary has become heavy. The leaden letters are starting to look like soldiers marching through my brain, digging around through my memories. I dare not even think how heavy it would be if I started writing down dreams.

Last night's dream weighed more than an ordinary day. Which is half a page. It may even weigh more than a shitty day. That's usually a page and seven or eight lines. I met a boy. We knew each other from a previous life. We knew everything about each other. Which side of the bed we liked to sleep on. The first song we remembered. The names of the trees which we used to climb as kids. He knew everything about me, but he wanted to hear about it anyway. It was as if he was seeing everything for the first time.

TO WANDER AND NOT TO BE LOST

Where do I start? It's good when you don't have a goal, it

means you can't get lost along the way. Every turn is a good
one. I think I read something like that in a book of Zen poetry.
Or was it *Alice in Wonderland*? I watched the store windows
and the blurry reflections of people passing by. Ghosts in the
glass. Trapped. I also look at the books in the store windows.
Shitty titles, by shitty authors, read by Philistines on public
transportation. Negative thoughts. Out. I'm looking for the
girl of my life.

SOMEWHERE BETWEEN

Do you see this?
　I see it.
　So, what do we do?
　Are we supposed to do something?
　Look, lately they've been messing up pretty bad there in
the bureaucracy of fate.
　So we're supposed to make it right?
　Well, yes.
　That's not our job, we're . . .
　Detectives, I know. But this looks like an interesting case.
　We shouldn't meddle.
　We won't, not directly.
　What do you suggest?
　An intermediary.
　Who do you have in mind?
　Pavel.
　But we already owe a favor to those guys.
　We'll take care of it somehow.
　What are you suggesting?
　We can sell them a couple of square miles of sky from their
age.

Isn't that too much?

They've been yearning for it for a long time, they keep staring at the sky.

Well, okay, as long as the bosses aren't on to us.

They won't be.

BEFORE THE SLEEP AND
THE MELTING GLACIERS

He left his lighter on the table. I'll give it back to him tomorrow when I see him. A couple of us are going on. He was in a bad mood, didn't want to come. *Tour de bars.* That's what it's called. In the next bar we run into a couple of journalist colleagues. From a different music website. A bit older. We beat them at basketball the other day. We tease them that they have to buy us beer. They do.

For the most part, we say nothing important; we talk about the new album of some band, and how it's not as good as the last one, it's just not rock 'n' roll anymore, they've gone soft, it's no good, man, fuck that polished production. Every other green beer bottle comes with a shot of wormwood schnapps, like a chorus follows a verse. One of my colleagues suggests that we move on, to the next bar. I said, sure.

Over there, everything stays the same. Bands, man, *Exile on Main St.* is one of the best rock 'n' roll albums of all times. Hell, it's probably the best. The Libertines saved our generation. The Arctic Monkeys have sold out, and Coldplay needs to be shot or publicly stoned. But I spot a girl over there, we slept together once, we were pretty drunk. We talk again, she, Iggy and I. I babble something about cultural studies, and she corrects me. It wasn't Stuart Hall who said that. Fuck, who did, then? Raymond Williams. Wait, doesn't he write detective novels? That's Raymond Chandler. Oh, yes, farewell, my lovely. Do you want to go to my place, she asks. I nod. Let's go, I say, just let me light another one. The fucking lighter doesn't work. I throw it away.

There, in her apartment, I sit on the floor, completely wasted. Her cat scratches at me and leaves hair all over my new pants. She plays some Neil Young. I feel a need to puke. I tell her that. She tells me to go to the toilet. I do. I splash some water on myself. I take a drink. Now only my head is spinning. I return to the room and collapse onto the mattress. The fucking cat pounces on me again. I'm going to go to sleep, I say. You're such an idiot, she says.

IN BETWEEN, ONCE AGAIN

Telephone booths are relics of a bygone age. Who the hell uses them anymore? We do. I enter a telephone booth. Hello, yes, put Pavel on the line. Hey, hello, pal. I need a favor. I know we owe you, but hear me out, I've got a good offer. A very good one. A couple of square miles of sky, what do you say? What kind of sky? What do you think? The kind that you're missing. Yes, listen to me, this is what's up, you need to get me a lighter. Why? So we can get the stars to align, that's how it goes, they don't align because of dramatic gestures, but with the little things. See, this lighter needs to reach this girl. Understood? Okay, great. Let me know when it's done.

CROWS AND LIGHTERS

Who does he think he is? An angel, yeah right. If all angels are such a pain in the ass, God help us. As if I've got nothing better to do than look for a lighter. That specific one. In a city of thousands (no, millions) of lighters, both thrown away and still alive. Impossible? Only if you are an amateur. But I'm not. I first hack into the neighborhood archives, find when the guy bought his last lighter. On his way into town. It didn't last long. And then I watch everywhere he went, think like he would think. I know all his favorite bars, I've checked all the files they have on him. That's the trickiest part, really. Angels can get all the files they need, no problem, but then their bosses will ask them what they need the files for. If the bosses realize that they've been messing with the bureaucracy of fate, all hell will break loose. That's where I come in. I can be lots of things. In the form of neon light, I disperse through the archives and find out everything I need. And now I'm a flash of wet tram tracks, gliding through the city. So, he was here first; okay, then he decided to head home. He must have left the lighter, so his buddy grabbed it. And then, all right, then they went on and it seems this guy was so drunk he couldn't light a cigarette, so he thought the lighter was broken. And, there it is. The flash of tracks reflects high into the sky and I turn into a crow. I grab the lighter in my beak. Now I just need to find her. Piece of cake.

I'M LATE, I'M SORRY

Even though she's gotten used to it, she shouldn't be okay with it. I'm a jerk, I admit it and I'm not trying to do anything about it. I'm selfish, I admit it and I'm not trying to do any-thing about it. I've decided not to try any harder than strictly necessary. And I can see her, she's reading a book. She's too nice to me, I know, and I should break up with her, but I've gotten used to care and patience. And I'm insecure. I'm so insecure.

I'm late, I know. I'm sorry.

That's okay.

Shall we?

Where to?

Wanna see a movie?

Nah, I don't feel like that today.

Wanna go for a walk?

It looks like it's going to rain, but it doesn't matter.

Let's go then.

Let's go.

THE LIGHTER

The fucking crow dropped me. It almost smashed me. Motherfucker.

THE WINDMILL

The night fell, the last daytime trams were headed to their des-tinations, and I hadn't found her. One by one the eyes of the skyscrapers went out; perhaps she was in one of them. And so I head to the square. With leaden steps and a frenzied stare. The night did a number on me. My dreams did a number on me. I follow the tracks, they seem to shine brighter than the streetlights. Perhaps I'll dream of her again. Perhaps this time I'll see her face.

THE LAST CIGARETTE

He's gone to meet his friends. I decided to go home. I gave him my lighter. That way I at least wouldn't smoke my last cigarette while waiting for the tram. I'll save it for the morning. I will light it on my gas stove. I shiver, watching the digital clocks on the tram terminal. I see a lighter on the ground and pick it up. It works. I decide to light a cigarette. Fuck it, I need some entertainment while I wait for that damn tram to come. A guy approaches me, looking like he's sleepwalking. He asks me if I've got a light. I tell him I do. He's silent for a couple of seconds. I realize I know him from before.

THE SKY

A package arrived, from the two detectives. We didn't know what to do with a piece of sky that large, so we installed it above our skyscraper. Above the neighborhood. A young sky above all that concrete and asphalt, above all those lives.

ONLY THE CIGARETTES WILL COST MORE

our pockets were empty, but our hearts were full . . .
—Nežni Dalibor

I'm not sure, but I think it was somewhere in the beginning of March that she said she was leaving, that she couldn't keep drinking with us and hearing again and again about the Japandroids and the Strokes, the future of rock 'n' roll and all tomorrow's parties. I took a sip from a plastic cup. A sip of cheap whiskey-cola, and I felt the electrons scurry hornily— no, nervously—along my body. She left for her apartment (luckily, it's not far away, and with a little bit of luck, her room-mate will not be home) where she will listen to the screaming of some lady singer, while the night screamed outside, and my electrons and nerves screamed along.

Is she mad at you? A friend asked, handing over what was left of the joint.

I shrugged and took the torch in my shivering, frozen fin-gers. The gust of smoke calmed the electrons down, made my nerves pulse on a different frequency, and above us the stars circled like tinfoil birds. On the park bench next to us, an underage girl was sitting on her boyfriend, straddling him with her legs, while his hands, his cold hands, crept up under her jacket and shirt; a bit further down in the distance, someone was pissing into the bushes, and even further off I could see someone rummaging through the trash, collecting bottles, their plastic bags filled to the brim; and my friend is talking to me, and I can hear him mention the new album by the Strokes, and how they sound like one of those mullet-headed crap bands from the eighties. I nod from time to time, saying that it sucks, how all those bands we had grown up on have gone to shit, but really all I can see is her, walking away, although her silhouette has gone around the corner a long time ago, but it seems to me I can still hear her footsteps rustling the fabric of the night; and so I drink, so—where was I—it seems like I'm flying, I'm crashing into a cloud, I'll take a leak on the rooftops.

Are you listening to me? A friend's voice comes from the other side of the ice, where the light is.

No, haven't been for a while.

Idiot.

I'll go to her.

Isn't she mad?

I don't know.

I'll see you.

You're staying?

There's still booze left.

Okay, bye.

I shivered my way to her house and kept ringing her intercom until she finally let me in. I couldn't find the lightswitch in the hallway so I started unsteadily climbing up the staircase. I realized I wasn't sure which floor her apartment was on. So I was standing there somewhere between the third and the fourth floor, breathing in the darkness, understanding that I understood nothing. A door opened on the floor below, puking lamplight over the hallway and stairwell, and in the doorway, she stood, sleepy, beautiful, and not at all eager for my company.

You're drunk.

You knew I was when you left.

Come on in.

I did.

Take off your shoes, I heard a voice from the kitchen.

Are you hungry?

No, I'm fine, I say hopping on one foot and trying to untie my laces, managing only to make an even bigger tangle. Frustrated, I try to pull them off and fall on the floor.

What was that? She says from the kitchen.

I've fallen.

Oh, okay then.

How is that okay? I think to myself. I finally manage to get my shoes off. I enter her room and collapse next to her on the mattress.

Go to sleep, she says.

And so I did. Dawn breaks at two in the afternoon, and she tells me she is leaving. She got a job in Luxembourg and wants me to go with her; the news seems somehow familiar to me, but I'm not sure when she mentioned it. I tell her that I don't see how this job is different from her current one. And everything is more expensive there, anyway.

You can't really intend to spend your life churning out music reviews and drinking at gas stations.

That hurt in several ways:

I don't churn them out, I *write* them.

And I don't only write reviews. I've written a novel. It just hasn't been published yet.

What's wrong with drinking at gas stations?

And then it hits me: her whole life, she has had goals that

are unfathomable and uninteresting, and I depend on my parents and the pittance I get for my reviews. And she'd like me to stop depending on my parents and start depending on her, just so she could, while I rub her feet after she comes home from work, complain that I spend all day doing nothing, playing my guitar, reading useless novels.

So, I come to some conclusions. Number one: I love her, even though I shouldn't. We hooked up during our first year at college. I didn't have a beard yet. She didn't have a job yet. I loved the Velvet Underground. She had a shirt with a banana on it. During our junior year at college, we moved into her apartment together, and I'd go to my parents' place every time her parents came to visit. Her father didn't like me. Her mother couldn't stand me. Physics is a tricky thing, all that inertia business. A relationship can take you far away, and suddenly you have no idea how you've ended up where you are, and you know that you wanted something different for yourself. Number two: she will leave me to be with someone from her line of work, and she will tailor her life perfectly. That at least is obvious. Our interests have been out of touch for a while now.

And finally, I don't know what your goals in life are. In fact, I don't know what it is exactly that you do. I don't know your favorite color or favorite flower or season, or your mother's maiden name or what your father does. I know you have twenty-seven birthmarks on your body, unless some of them got scratched off, and that you like to say the word *crispy*, and that you like *the ocean*, and that you used to want to write, but would say that there wasn't any language that would allow you to express everything you saw. I tried to invent one. I can tell what you're dreaming about by the way you breathe and curl up your toes. Those aren't important things, I'm aware of that, but nobody else knows them.

So, what do you say?

To what?

To the plan.

I'm not sure.

What do you mean? You of all people always talk about escaping from this city.

I'm not sure that going to Luxembourg, where you've got a job, is my escape. At least, that's not how I see escape. In any case, what would I do up there? I . . .

You don't have a job.

I don't.

So find one.

As if it's that easy.

Well, have you ever tried it?

I've had no reason to.

What about my job?

I'm happy with my job here.

That can hardly be called a job.

Oh really? Let's see you write ten pages about the new music scene in the region.

I don't care about that.

I don't care about your stuff.

My stuff?

Yeah. Whatever it is that you do.

Whatever it is?

Right.

Do you even know what I do?

You've got a real job.

A real job?

Like, you sit and work, punch in your hours, that's it.

Excuse me?

Nothing ever changes.

And your writing changes the world?

No, but it changes my consciousness—I had to laugh because that simply wasn't true. I am not an ambitious guy. I used to be. But my ambitions weren't profitable.

Oh come on, please. You're just scared to make an effort.

I've written a novel.

That nobody published.

That took more courage than just doing a job.

How so? Because not getting published has trampled over your pride?

I shut up. How can I explain to her that I don't mind being useless, that I still have romantic illusions about the world, and that I am not a man who wants to join the rat race and fit his life into a briefcase? At least, that's how I see it. I don't want to have a boss. I don't want to work for someone else. I don't believe in a better future, I don't believe in a promised land. Anyway, a promised land awaits us as well. I remember talking to her about it. I told her that, in the promised land, the politicians will wear the same suits. Only the cigarettes will cost more. And the bills will have a different color. The rules of the game will stay the same. It was never about me being too dumb to follow the rules. The rules are very simple. Brutal and simple. It's just that I liked another game better. One that was more like hopscotch and skipping rope. But I've forgotten the rules to those games. I was stuck in the limbo of adolescence.

So, what now? She asks me.

I don't know.

When will you know?

I don't know.

That's your answer to everything.

Maybe.

I'm taking the job.

Okay.

Okay?

Okay.

Silence again.

I don't know, I tell her.

What now?

How did we get here? How come we never noticed before that each of us has been pulling in his own direction?

I've been pulling, you're just a slob I haven't been able to budge.

We laugh.

What now, then?

I asked you that just a moment ago.

I know.

You know?

I know.

So, what now?

I'll think about it, I lie.

And then I left. And then she left. First she left me, then she left the country. That night I dreamt the sound of railroad tracks. But she doesn't like trains. A couple of months later, we joined the promised land. Until then, I wandered desolate landscapes like a drunken Moses, waiting for manna to fall from the sky. I had been right. Almost nothing changed. The bills have a different color. The cigarettes are more expensive. I smoke a pack a day, just like before. I'm just a bit thinner.

THIS ONE'S ON THE ANGELS

for seven days they walked, their heads
bathing and diving in the darkness
on the eighth morning,
the plain opened up before them
　　　　　　　　　　　—Rešicki

The angels sat at the bar, enveloped in their blurry auras. An unskilled observer would have called it a trick of dim bar lights and smoke. He wouldn't have a clue. They were angels, sitting at the bar. And what of the devils? For some, they were trapped at the bottom of their glasses; for others, in their heads. It's all in your head, buddy, a wise man used to tell me. An interesting bunch they are, angels, demons, and wise men. The only thing lacking is prophets. Some drunk will claim that title for himself soon enough, we just have to wait. Real prophets are all but gone; they're mostly fucked up, broken, insane.

I was waiting for Maroje. He would recognize them. I took a sip of beer and started tapping my fingers against the table. Maroje came in, glancing nervously around, looking for me. That unnerving moment while you look for your people. He notices me, takes off his coat, and sits opposite me.

Fuck, it's freezing outside, he says.

I nod towards the bar.

He turns around to take a look.

Angels?

Yeah. I knew you'd spot them.

How couldn't I? With their aura of pathos.

Where are Marin and the others?

They're going to a party, two or three blocks away.

What are we waiting for, then?

My beer.

Who's going to be there?

I don't know, but I've heard that there's people there who know you.

As long as there's girls there . . .

*

The shadows flicker on the walls, over the faces, on the bodies. It's difficult to breathe. Used-up air. Gone through many lungs. We can't reach the bar through the crowd. I say that to Maroje. He lights a cigarette and steps forward. He uses the tip of his cigarette to pierce the crowd. The bodies move out of the way. Maroje is the Moses of nightclubs. We reach the bar. I see many familiar faces. Some are older than they were when I last saw them. They've learned a couple of life lessons. Beer and honey schnapps. Guaranteed to get the job done. Maks is there as well. Maks plays the lead guitar in an underground band.

Hey, Maks, what's up?

Nothing, man, there're more people here than I thought would come.

That's good, right?

Yeah, but now I can't reach the bar.

You've got existential problems to deal with, I can see.

Shut up. Have you seen Nikolina?

Nikolina?

LAST NIGHT   161

From your high school.

Oh. No, I haven't. Why?

She's so fucked up.

Why?

She's wasted already. She's lost it, I tell you. She goes out every day.

What, she's got problems?

Obviously. With herself.

Oh. Okay, Maks, see you later.

Bye.

Maroje says he will step out to get some air. I turn around. I look for Nikolina. No need. She approaches me. I can't hear her, so I lean in. I can feel her breath on my neck.

Hey, hi.

Hi, Nikolina.

Long time no see.

Another country, another crowd. That's how it goes.

Yeah, I've heard you've been to Germany. Why did you come back?

A change of surroundings is not the same as a change of skin.

No, but it's a good start.

True. And you? What have you been up to?

Surviving. Breaking stuff.

That's good. Surviving is what's important.

You know, I really liked your poetry. A sudden change of topic.

Liked it? Why the past tense?

Well, I haven't read any of your poems in a long while.

I don't write them as often as I used to.

Too bad. Why?

I can't.

You can't?

No.

Nonsense.

Would you like a drink? I change the subject.

I wouldn't mind a vodka.

I order vodka for us. At that moment, Maks approaches us. Shows us he's got some pills. We follow him into the bathroom. He crushes the pills under a glass. Nikolina and I pour them into our vodkas; Maks pours them into his beer. We drink up. We don't feel a thing. I keep talking to Nikolina, I don't know about what, probably our writing. I only know that she is too close to me, and that her face is no longer playful like it was in high school. I don't feel any closeness. I don't tell her that. Her face is no longer playful, I don't know why. Something has happened to her. I don't know what. It seems like someone has torn her out of the room. She is completely cut off from the bodies around her. The shadows slide from the walls. They shimmer on her face. I can't see the color of her eyes. Green? No. No, not green. The shadows are around us now. We are no longer in the club, and I don't know where we are going. Maks is talking about Joy Division..

....

Nikolinastealingbeersintheclub. Not in the one where we were before. This one has people in expensive suits. A lot of familiar faces. We've grown a bit older. We think we know what life is about. We're dumb. Aus Frankfurt? Ach, so. Ich lebte in Münster. And I don't know how, but suddenly we're all alone. Nikolina, Maks, Maroje, and myself. Just us and the angels. Maroje tells us that this round is on them. And so we fall, piercing the clouds. Nothing hurts anymore, and everything is carefree.

*

The sky in my dream was red. When I woke up, the dreams hung dispersed in the air for a long time. I threw up. I decided to sleep through the day.

*

17:11 I'm never drinking again.

*

23:08 I should write something about the dream and my night out

*

00:14 still no idea for a story

*

01:54 good night.

RED SHIFT, PART TWO

These goalposts were placed here with skilled players in mind.

Why do you say that?

Look at the fence.

It was a green wire fence behind the goal.

So?

Think about it. Ten meters wide, six meters high. If I'm going to miss, it won't be just by ten meters wide and six meters high.

Makes sense.

Maroje and I were standing on the centerline of a football field, on a school playground, facing the goals, talking about everything and nothing. Our breath fogged up in the cold, we stuck our hands down our jacket pockets and remarked that the sky was the same color as the concrete. Maroje and I have the same majors. People already have a habit of mentioning us in the same sentences.

You looked shaken yesterday, Maroje says, kicking a pebble at the goal. He doesn't miss.

Oh really? I mumble, picking at a hangnail on my thumb with my nail.

Yes, when we were down at the Sling.

I wasn't shaken. Okay, maybe just a bit.

What happened?

Nikolina.

You and Nikolina hardly ever talk anyway.

I think she hardly ever talks to anyone.

Why do you think so?

Man, did you take a good look at her yesterday?

No, why?

I've known Nikolina since high school. I liked her at first, but she was dating some schmuck. I ran into him later, in college. He was still a schmuck. Nikolina is a short, pretty girl; her long brown hair looks wild, even though she combs it, and her curious eyes, like a newborn's, carefully observe her surroundings. She's got good legs. That's what Maroje remembered her by. For a time, we couldn't stand each other, I was told. I met her last night at the Sling. Last night her eyes didn't shine with curiosity in the darkness of the club. She was with her gang. We exchanged a couple of sentences. In a drunken voice, she told me she liked my poems and that she would love to read some new ones. The tone of her voice and the rhythm in which she spoke told me something was not right.

Her smile was like an empty amusement park. There was a distance in her eyes, as if she wasn't in the room at all.

I've heard that, if you want to end up with her, it's enough to just stand next to her.

She's dealing with something.

And you, Sherlock, you can tell from her eyes.

I ran into Nikolina several times after that, each time in a dark club. It was during my first or second year of college, and I knew a lot of people from her crowd, and I even started a band with one of them. That was how I started hanging out with them. After several years of being acquaintances, I finally got to know Nikolina better. She read a lot. She loved to talk about the universe; about the future, not so much.

Yeah, I don't like to talk about the future either, we're not on a first-name basis, I told her once, trying to sound like a rebel. Actually, I was horribly worried about the future and suffered from a need to overanalyze and dissect my feelings, sentences, words, gestures and dreams. With her, I stopped doing that. She reminded me about the rules of the game, not to take myself too seriously.

She simply said the future wasn't what it used to be. At that moment it seemed like the sentence I had been trying to write for a long time. I realized that everything I had typed in God-knows-how-many sentences can be condensed into that one. We were lying in my bed and we could only see the outlines of the room. I felt her warm breath on my cheek, and her finger gliding across my chest.

Do you still write poetry?

Yes, but nowadays I'm more into prose.

Would you like to publish a book?

I nodded. She kissed my neck.

If I wrote, I'd finish every chapter with a comma,

*

Sometimes I feel like an encyclopedia of useless knowledge. For example, I know that Constantinople was conquered in 1453, that Guy Stevens produced *London Calling*, I know that *Darklands* by The Jesus and Mary Chain was on the 1987 best-of-the-year list of our socialist youth magazine, *Polet*. I know that, if I'm going to meet Nico at eight, the bus arrives at 19:49. I regularly run two or three minutes late. I know she won't get mad, but that doesn't make the cut for the encyclope-dia of useless knowledge. The fact that Miroslav Krleža loved to drink the Blatina wine will, as will the fact that, in a scene in *Coffee and Cigarettes*, Iggy Pop is playing from the jukebox.

At the Spanish Bar in Soho, the jukebox has Sid Vicious's version of "My Way." A graffiti in the underpass connecting my neighborhood of Utrine with its three neighbors says that *the night is colder than outside*. It got painted over. Soon afterwards, the same graffiti appeared. I no longer found it funny.

Maroje and I were sitting on the crossbar of a goal at the school playground. The sky wasn't the color of concrete. It was blue, but not a summery blue. In the summer, the sky looks closer. He asked me how I knew that, and I told him my work desk was next to the window, so I spent too much time staring through it. He asked me if I knew all the shades of the sky. I didn't. But the Sahara sky was my favorite.

You've never been to the Sahara.

I've never been, but you know when the sky gets almost gold, and then morphs into purple? Celestial alchemy.

Perhaps I should spend more time looking at the street, at the passersby, the kids in the park. One could write about that as well.

Once I've written everything I can about the sky, I'll move on to the streets.

*

Maroje and I drank too much those days. You could talk to him about all the important things. About music, poetry, and prose, the madness of the West and the idea of escape. And like I said, we drank too much those days. I still claim it was because we read more than a thousand pages a week. The night strewn across the sky, a couple of bottles, our insanity, and the insanities of the authors whose lines we read.

We agreed that the world had become like *Catch-22*. Like a *Monty Python* sketch. Like one of Bukowski's surreal, desolate dreams. We had seen the ads offering surgical procedures with a seaside view, flyers for gurus and swamis who had all the solutions and correct answers. And the masses kept gobbling them up. The writers no longer needed to make these things up. The age of the absurd was in front of us, underneath us, inside us.

*

Nikolina's mind is an abyss. Nikolina's mind sometimes scares me. I don't know what devils plague her, what deformed memories haunt her. I can only hear the echoes. I don't remember clearly, but I think we broke up three times last night. The next morning we gathered the evidence—and our clothes across the apartment. A bra hanging from a lamp, scarves tangled on the floor, coats in front of the apartment door. The next morning that fragmented night seemed so distant, so surreal, like the lives of others. She put on my shirt and combed her hair. I made coffee. We said that we would talk about last night's pandemonium. We didn't have anything to say. With Nico I decided to decipher silence, and words unspoken.

Nikolina's mind is an abyss. Nikolina's mind fascinates me, and every once in a while I walk up to the edge of the cliff and stare into the blackness. I've realized that there's moments when I consider free-falling, accepting this madness.

Wow hare you? She interrupts my musings.

Geelin' food.

Fying, you lool.

Twy hwalk thike lis?

Bo dreak the doring boutine.

Geelin' food. Lot nying.

Ut shup and kive me a giss.

I did. It was soft. Like snow.

*

I lead several lives at once. Two or three years ago I was exposed to solitude for the first time. I spent a couple of months in Münster, a small university town in Germany near the Dutch border. That's where I learned to wander. I wrote down dozens of stories in my mind, and in the notebook I carried everywhere. I learned to appreciate solitude and, more importantly, I learned to observe the world around me and the world within me. I realized that there were stories in all of us, unbelievable, amazing stories, that every person contained thousands of unwritten pages. As children, we fantasize about adventures and castles in the clouds; when we grow up, we fantasize about escape. It's not true that kids have better imaginations; it's just that, when we get slightly older, we're told that no future can be built on idleness and imagination. They got it into our heads that a safe future is better than a rich present, and that is how we lose our innocence. Not through sin, but through oblivion, through abandoning the heaven we were born with.

What happens to our abandoned dreams? To the world in which we were heroes, children of promise?

With each thought we create a new world. It is never abandoned, it goes on living regardless of whether we've forgotten about it in this world, Nico tells me.

What about us?

Which us?

Those whose thoughts give life to those worlds. Do they live forever?

Of course, we never die.

I think I've heard that somewhere before.

In another life?

I don't remember past lives. Anyways, I may not have heard it anywhere, I may have come up with it myself.

It does sound like something you would say.

It sounds like something both of us would say.

And the things I say, how do they sound?

They sound true. Sometimes a bit sad.

You don't know me well enough yet.

In fact, I don't know her at all, and I'm not sure if anyone knows her. Nikolina will remain an undreamt dream.

*

Nico wrote as well. She was pretty good. Unlike most young writers, she didn't have a problem with her ego. Her stories perfectly manifested her inner chaos. They maintained a courteous distance from reality. I never tried to find my own face in her stories. I wasn't that selfish.

*

It was Christmas Day, or a day of that sort. I remember it was Friday, or maybe Tuesday, but that doesn't matter. Once again, we found ourselves in the dark of a nightclub. Nico, me, and the rest of the crowd. I don't remember the details, but I remember Nico, drunk as she was, hallucinating that Frederic Beigbeder was there, and introducing herself to him. She said he paid her two beers.

I was in the bathroom at the time, trying my best not to piss on everything around me. Hearing the sloshing of the water, like a steadfast captain I steadied the course, trying not to stumble. I failed. I pissed myself a bit. Doesn't matter, in the dark of the club nobody would notice. I walked out of the bathroom and headed toward Nico. As soon as she saw me, she started kissing me; I didn't complain. In the middle of our kiss, I took the glass of whiskey from her hand; she didn't complain.

*

Where does the sky begin? I roll a joint. I do so poorly. Jura is on the wall. Jura is a spider.

Just a couple of inches outside your reach. Nikolina always takes so long to get out of bed.

That's sad. But I wasn't talking to you.

To who, then?

Jura.

Your spider?

He's not MY spider. He's his own man.

He's a spider.

You know what I mean.

What would you do with the sky, anyway, if you could reach it?

I'd take a piece of it for myself.

Play hopscotch, that way you're sure to get up there.

I don't know if I want to.

You just said . . .

. . . that's not me anymore.

Oh. Okay then.

We associated steadiness with boredom. I don't know when those two terms became synonymous for us, but Nico thinks that this isn't really normal, and that it has happened because we've never been faced with bigger problems. She had trouble defining "bigger problems."

Anyway, I say while I finish rolling the joint, it's enough to be able to look at the sky.

And that is best done while lying down, she said and stretched in the bed.

I don't know, really, the way you're lying down, you can only see the ceiling.

Why don't you light that joint and we'll pretend that the smoke is a cloud.

I lie down next to her and light up. The smoke snakes through my airways. I cough, and my eyes well up. I take a couple more hits and hand her the joint. The ashes scatter across the bed. Jura has buggered off somewhere. We bore him.

You know, we can't go on like this forever, she says between hits.

Why not? I love rolling around with you and making up new words for things like "lying in the shade of a tree" or "lying down and staring at the ceiling."

The Japanese have a word for that.

For staring at the ceiling? Or for lying in the shade of a tree?

No, for watching a cherry tree blossom. *Hanami.*

Huh, and *hanabi* means "fireworks."

Yeah, anyway, we can't go on like this forever.

I wouldn't change a single woe of today for all the empires of tomorrow. I think Šoljan said that.

I don't mean it like that. You know, I sometimes feel like you're not all there.

Maybe it was not Šoljan, but it doesn't sound like Slamnig.

Sometimes you're so intoxicated by the moment that you're not there anymore; you're too busy thinking of how you're going to commit that moment to paper.

Oh, right, Mihalić, of course. It was Mihalić who said it.

Sometimes it's okay to be boring. Not every moment is poetry.

I fall silent. I turn to the side and put my arms around Nikolina. The touch of naked skin. We decide to sleep through the day.

*

I give her my sailor shirt. She looks good in it.

*

Night by night, it keeps getting worse. Every morning I count the dead, every morning there is a new voice in my head. They're conspiring against me, the voices. They've decided to drive me insane. By doubt. By questioning. By creating scenarios of hypothetical situations. By reminding me of missed opportunities. I wasn't able to get out of bed, I gave up halfway there. Through the gaps in the shelf above my bed, lying on my back, I managed to stare at the sky, straight at the blue morning. Actually, it was noon, but I liked the image of a blue morning, of a world that was turned upside down because of my current position.

Nico had gone home a couple of hours ago, and I had shifted to her side of the bed; it was warm and smelled of her. There was really no need to get out of bed. I lay with my eyes closed, trying to fall asleep, but instead of sleep, my eyelids were overcome by a cramp. I shut them so hard it hurt. And slowly the chill crept up, a feeling like a hedgehog climbing from your stomach to your heart.

We agreed to give ourselves some time, think about it and then decide what to do. She said that there was no point in repeating the same scenario every night, saying the same things to each other, spitting out words that only leave a bitter taste in our mouths. I already knew what I was going to tell her. Unfortunately, I was an idiot in love. A nasty situation. She was being rational, and I was in denial. A dumb man and a *femme fatale*: a match made in heaven.

*

We broke up. She broke up with me, more precisely. She said my problem was that I lived in words. She said that she was kind of crazy. She said that she needed to deal with some things on her own. I still haven't formed a plan for next week. Curling up under a blanket seems like a very good solution. But the only thing worse than dreaming about Nico is waking up without her. I've decided to change my sheets, they smelled like her too much.

*

Maroje called me today. He asked how I felt.
    Like shit.
    Let's go drinking.
    That was his answer for everything. A practical man.

*

My mother brought me soup in bed. She asked me if I was going out. I told her to close the blinds. I drank the soup and went back to sleep.

*

My father finally got tired of my lounging around and

self-pitying. I tried to explain to him that I enjoyed floating around in oceans of despair and narcissistic laments, and he told me to go and take my ass outside. So I found myself in the cold. Helpless as a newborn and equally confused and disarmed. I screamed, but no one cared. The sun's rays beat down on my back at a speed of 186,000 miles per second, there were no clouds in the sky, and the birds were singing. I raised the collar of my coat, stuffed my hands into my pockets and headed somewhere, anywhere. I reached the green fence of a schoolyard. When I was a child, that line represented a boundary I wasn't allowed to cross. It was the edge of the world, the end of civilization; who knew what was out there, under that foreign sky? I realized it was time for me to find out.

This sentence is a good way to end this manuscript.

SVEN POPOVIĆ was born on September 19, 1989 in Zagreb, in the part of Yugoslavia now known as Croatia. His short stories were published in the anthology of young Croatian writers (*Bez vrata, bez kucanja*, Sandorf 2012), in a collection of short stories *Record Stories* (Aquarius Records, 2011), and in various magazines and webzines like *Quorum*, *Zarez*, and *Arteist*. As a freelance journalist, he has contributed to several magazines such as *Zarez*, *Aktual*, and the Austrian leftist magazine *Wespennest*, as well as writing literary and album reviews for various webzines. His collection of short stories, *Last Night* (Meandarmedia) came out in 2015 and received excellent reviews. Several of his stories were included in *Best European Fiction 2017* (Dalkey Archive Press). His first novel, *Uvjerljivo drugi*, was published in 2018, and his second, *Mali i Levijatan*, in 2024.

VINKO ZGAGA has translated several plays for stage production, including Tennessee Williams's *Orpheus Descending* (2008), Christopher Durang's *The Marriage of Bette and Boo* (2009), and Simon Stephens's *Light Falls* (2022). He has a long-standing working relationship with the Croatian Centre of the International Theatre Institute, having translated many plays for their Croatian Theatre Showcase event and the texts of several Croatian authors into English, including Dino Pešut's play *Static*, Mate Matišić's trilogy *Wax People*, and Sven Popović's short-story collection *Last Night*.

Printed in the USA
CPSIA information can be obtained
at www.ICGtesting.com
JSHW080522260924
70407JS00001B/1

9 781628 975000